Margaret Killjoy

A COUNTRY OF GHOSTS

BLACK DAWN SERIES

"This gritty evocative novel explores the question of what an anarchist community can do to resist the assaults that are sure to come if any such social formation were to exist. Yet more important still is that this is an exciting and mysterious novel, a story of war and love in some fictional mountainous country with echoes of nineteenth century Latin America, eastern Europe, central Asia; by the time you're done you feel you've gotten a glimpse into a forgotten part of our history that is nevertheless very real." —Kim Stanley Robinson, author of the *Mars* trilogy

"An epic political fantasy in the tradition of Tepper and Le Guin—there is no writer working today quite like Margaret Killjoy. A brave, unapologetic, and fiercely original book" —Laurie Penny, author of *Everything Belongs to the Future*

"*A Country of Ghosts* is entertaining, its politics intriguing, and the setting is a place I found myself missing after I turned the last page." —Nick Mamatas, author of *I am Providence* and *Bullettime*.

"This is a fierce, intelligent, hopeful book—a fantasy (of sorts) of unusual seriousness, humanity, and wit." —Felix Gilman, author of *The Half-Made World*

"*Gulliver's Travels* meets *The Dispossessed*. It's a wild ride, and you don't want to miss it." —Gabriel Kuhn, author of *Life Under the Jolly Roger*

With the Black Dawn series we honor anarchist traditions and follow the great Octavia E. Butler's legacy, Black Dawn seeks to explore themes that do not reinforce dependency on oppressive forces (the state, police, capitalism, elected officials) and will generally express the values of antiracism, feminism, anticolonialism, and anticapitalism. With its natural creation of alternate universes and world-building, speculative fiction acts as a perfect tool for imagining how to bring forth a just and free world. The stories published here center queerness, Blackness, antifascism, and celebrate voices previously disenfranchised, all who are essential in establishing a society in which no one is oppressed or exploited. Welcome, friends, to Black Dawn!

BLACK DAWN SERIES #2

SANINA L. CLARK, SERIES EDITOR

The below addresses would be delighted to provide you with the latest AK Press distribution catalog, which features books, pamphlets, zines, and stylish apparel published and/or distributed by AK Press. Alternatively, visit our websites for the complete catalog, latest news, and secure ordering.

AK Press	AK Press
370 Ryan Ave. #100	33 Tower Street
Chico, CA 95973	Edinburgh, Scotland EH6 7BN
www.akpress.org	akuk.com

Cover art by Juan Carlos Barquet, www.jcbarquet.com
Cover design and logo by T. L. Simons, tlsimons.com
Map illustrated by Eno Farley
Printed in the USA

For Kate. This whole utopia thing was her idea anyhow.

Acknowledgments

A single person does not write a book. These pages wouldn't exist without: Kate, for explaining why utopia matters and a million other reasons. Parks, for telling me what happens when people get shot and cut up. Melissa, for telling me about horses. Miriam and Kelley and Maria and April, for the feedback. The Catastrophone Orchestra, without whom the plot would have been much worse. Amy, for the encouragement. Ceightie, because always. Ben, for explaining what freedom means. John, for explaining half of what I know about economics. My family, because they're my family. Kelsey, for talking about what it means to be an anarchist fighting for your country. Whoever wrote the zine *Orc*, for caring about fantasy and understanding why it matters. Ursula K. Le Guin, Starhawk, and Graham Purchase, for exploring this terrain before me. The Bugaboo, Delta Loop, Artnoose, and everyone else who has housed a nomadic writer. Leviathan, my machine, my comrade.

Despite the expert advice I received from so many, any mistakes and oversimplifications are completely my own.

A COUNTRY OF
GHOSTS

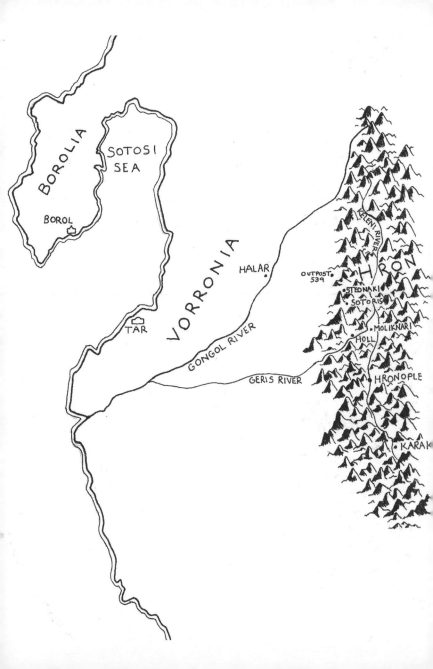

One

"The Man Beneath the Top Hat" is what I thought I was going to call the series, back when the editors of the *Borol Review* first assigned it to me. Forty, maybe fifty column inches a week for six months on Dolan Wilder, "the man who conquered Vorronia." Dolan Wilder, the enigmatic young upstart of His Majesty's Imperial Army, famous for his bold, ride-at-the-front-of-the-charge style. The man who put more square miles under the gold-and-green than anyone had in a century.

I was all set to write about his rough-shaven face, his black locks, his fine taste in brandy, and the soft touch he had for granting quarter to conquered foes. I was told at least two column inches were reserved for his gruff-but-friendly tone. I was to write about a cold, stony man who nursed a tender heart that beat only for service, only for the King, only for the glory of the Borolian Empire.

Instead, though, I saw him die. But no matter, that—he bore few of those traits I'd been told to ascribe to him, and bore none of them well. Instead I write to you of Sorros Ralm, a simple militiaman, and of the country of Hron. And it seems you won't find my report in the *Review*.

....

For a writer of my adventurous temperament and immodest ambition, it was a dream assignment. I can't tell you I wasn't elated when Mr. Sabon, my editor, called me into his smokey office and told me I'd been sent to the front, to be embedded in Wilder's honor guard.

"I'll be honest with you, Dimos," Mr. Sabon said to me, breathing shallow in that strange, wounded way of his, "you're not getting this job because we think you're the best. You're not. You're getting this job because it's important but dangerous, and you're the best writer we can afford to lose."

"I understand," I replied, because I did. My middling place in the stable of writers had been made clear to me near-daily since my demotion.

"I know you like to tell the truth," he continued. "You're an honest man. And that's fine—we're an honest paper. But I don't want you stirring anything up just for the sake of stirring it up."

"I understand," I said.

"I mean it. Look me in the eye and tell me all that's behind you."

"It is," I said. And at the time, I'm pretty sure I meant it.

"Good," he said. "Because this is an important assignment, real important. You do this, and everyone in this city is going to know your name."

That much, at least, was true.

....

I walked out of his office with my head held as high as my spirits, floated down the stairs, and returned to my desk in the pool of hacks. I put on my bowler and coat and walked out of that building and onto the streets of Borol, the low winter sun failing as always to bring even a hint of warmth through the chill fog that rolled off the bay and stunk of industry.

I took more mind of the city that day than most, knowing I was soon to depart. I was off to the savage wilds, to the very edge of empire and civilization, to leave behind the comforts and sanity of His Majesty's capital city. Not ten feet from the door, I tripped over an urchin girl passed out from hunger or vice.

I know most of my readers will be well-acquainted with the conditions of the working and middle class of Borol, so I won't linger too long on the details of that walk, but I hope you will indulge me a bit as it serves such an amazing contrast to Hron, to the world I did not yet know I was off to see.

My walk took me through the docks and their attendant horrors of press gangs and bribed officials, through the meatpacking district and the human screams that were so often indistinguishable from the death cries of slaughtered beasts. I walked through Strawmarak Square, where the nobility and merchant houses attend theatre, defended from the protestations of the poor by means of policemen with sticks and guns. I walked the edge of Royal Park, where, scattered among the birch groves, were the lot who'd been left with little to sell but sex and had nowhere safe to do so. I walked past men at work and men without work, past children playing games like "nick a wallet or you won't eat tonight," past barkers and buskers and scavengers and skips, past cripples and beggars and whores, past dandies and gang fights, past lamentations and sorrow and the strange joy one finds in the daftest of places.

In short, I walked through Borol. And I didn't suppose I would miss it.

....

I was month-to-month at my rooming house, so packing up meant saying goodbye to my tiny apartment. To be honest, that wasn't very hard—it's been a long time since I've been sentimental about where I sleep. And I owned almost nothing, as my room had come furnished and I got my books from the library.

My three suits went into my steamer trunk—I doubted I'd have a chance to wear them where I was going, but I had nowhere to leave them anyway. My underclothes and most of the rest of my personal effects filled the rest of the trunk.

In my satchel, I put tobacco and pipe; a journal; my travel documents; and, wrapped up in the cotton kerchief that was all that remained of my mother, a set of brass knuckles. It might have been like bringing a knife to a gunfight, but the solid weight felt like more than enough with which to take on the world.

....

Truth be told, it was to be my first time off the peninsula. I'd been a reporter for five of the twenty-three years I'd been alive, but here's how colonial reporting was done at the *Review*: I sat at a desk and read Morse code off the wire. Sure, I spoke four languages, and sure, I took raw data and used it to write what I hoped were compelling, informative narratives, but there was a reason they called us hacks. Nearly all of our foreign correspondents were rather domestic.

The Chamber of Expansion itself was underwriting the story on Wilder, so I had an economy cabin aboard the *HMR Tores*, a double-wide luxury train that ran the overland route to the mainland. It was the long way to Vorronia, to be sure, but the Council had provided me with no small amount of reading material and the extra few days gave me time to pour through the tens of thousands of words already put into ink regarding the exploits of our hero Wilder.

I spent the hour of daylight that remained watching as the famous idyll of the Borolian countryside swept past my window, then turned my attentions to the task before me.

"Our country is in peril," my assignment from the Council began. "Popular support for expansionist policy is flagging, leaving us vulnerable."

The council went on to explain that, ever since Vorronia had acquiesced to our rule and signed the Sotosi Treaty, recruitment had been down. There was a whole page about how the Cerrac mountains were rich with iron and coal, and a second about how it was our duty to bring the fruits of civilization to the few scattered villages and towns in the area. What the country needed was a hero to inspire recruitment, the Council explained, a hero like Wilder.

"The Man Beneath the Top Hat" was born in poverty and dragged himself out of the mire with hard work, patriotism, and a gravely voice that demanded respect, reaching the rank of General Armsman by force of will and valor alone. And I had three thick books in my luggage that could prove it.

It's hard to remember how I'd felt about the assignment at the time. I'd like to say I'd known it was all so much horseshit. I'd written probably a thousand column inches in the *Review* about the conditions that the majority of Borolians lived in, back before they put me to staffing the wire, and I didn't think the Vorronian war had done anything for them but killed those fool enough to enlist or unlucky enough to be conscripted. Victory, unsurprisingly enough, hadn't brought a one of the corpses back to life.

But I admit that I'd probably thought this was different. We weren't fighting a war, we were colonizing the mountains. We were guaranteeing the country access to resources.

And it wasn't my job to editorialize. I'd tried that once, had maybe oversimplified some things, and I'd seen with my own eyes the damage self-righteous reporting can wreak. So I didn't think it was my place as a journalist to question the story itself, the story that ran all the way to the roots of the Empire. I didn't question the story that of course we had a king, that of course we obeyed the Chambers and their attendant police. Of course we worked for the expansion of imaginary lines, of course we let industrialists amass wealth.

So I was probably just excited to have been given such an important assignment.

....

In my four days on the *Tores* I ate more money's worth of food than I had in the rest of my life up to that point all told. I was fed delicacies from the colonies and elsewhere around the world: stuffed red swan from Zandia, rainbow caviar from the Floating Isles, wildfruit cobbler from Ora, live-fried eel from Vorronia, sprouted godleaf from Dededeon, the list goes on.

Even at the time, I knew what was happening. I was being bribed, teased by a taste of the upperclass life. The Chamber of Expansion was trying to win me over, and they wanted me to write about their generosity. Even more so, they wanted me to write of their fine taste. Because even if I wrote about the decadent luxury of the aristocracy with the intent of fueling class hatred, the story would still be "the rich have fine taste. You should want the things that only imperial society can grant you."

So yes, I drank their scotch and brandy, ate their exotic foods.

These things were passable. Delectable, even. But, then, I used to think the measure of a food was found in its richness and rarity.

. . . .

I read every one of those books, for what it's worth. But I feel no need to repeat what I learned of Dolan Wilder here. There's enough propaganda in Borol about the man, and I feel no need to add to it.

. . . .

We pulled into Tar just after dawn, the train clanging south along the isthmus. The sun rose over the bay and cast the train's long shadow over the Sotosi Sea. I had a tranquil moment then, looking out over that expanse of red water. The tide was an iron-and-blood shade of crimson, and it was hard not to think about the decades of war and the hundreds of thousands of people who had bled out into or drowned in those waters. It's the algae, not the blood, that turns the tide red of course, but the algae feeds on blood.

I tried to see Borolia, but there's not a spyglass in the world that could have let me see my home a hundred miles across that water.

I'd written uncountable words about Tar, the capital city of Vorronia. For two years I wrote about the war there, following the front as it advanced and withdrew, and I knew the street map of the place by heart. For three years after that I wrote about peace there, and I knew more about the factory strikes and the reimposition of child labor by colonial forces than, I would guess, the average citizen of Tar. But I was not arrogant enough to say that I knew the city. A city is more than a map of battles and it is more than its news.

I can't describe what it was like to pull into King's Station (née

Pior Station) and see the iron palisades, to walk out onto King's Square (née Vorros Square) and look out on the steel-clad, eight-masted palace ship, moored in the bay, stationary now for 450 years, attached to the shore as much by polished barnacle as by chain and rope. I knew all of these things would be waiting for me, but they were not *quite* as I had pictured them in my head for the past five years of my life. It was uncanny, unnerving, and absolutely beautiful.

There in Tar, my assignment was a mixed blessing. It was being sent to the front that had brought me to the city of my dreams, but it was my duty to a group of men I didn't even much respect to catch the next train for the front. There I was in Vorronia, but no matter how much I longed to walk the canals, to flirt with gup-pymen and test my Vorronian sailor slang in the aviary bars of the gull district, I couldn't.

I took in the ambience of King's Square—the scents of herb bread and piss, the cries of gulls and sparrows—and then turned sharply on my heel and marched back into King's Station. I found a seat on a stone bench, waited an hour, then boarded a train headed east from Tar. I fumed.

The Chamber had wined and dined me on the *Tores*, but that was the last comfort they were to extend to me. I was to take that regional train for eighteen hours, out to the end of its line. To Outpost 539—an evocative name, that. There, I was told, someone or other would meet me and we'd make the last leg of our journey by carriage.

No longer granted a cabin, I took my seat on the aisle next to a Vorronian woman maybe five or ten years older than myself. I envied her the window view, and spent most of the day watching farms rush past. Many of them had been abandoned to the wild, and even the inhabited ones were clearly falling into disrepair. Grapes flowed over their trellises unchecked, and green flower creeping-vine had swallowed entire buildings.

My seatmate noticed me looking, and I was grateful she recognized I was staring at the countryside and not at her.

"This is your fault," she said in her own language, with none of the characteristic Vorronian politeness I'd so often read about.

"I'm sorry," I replied, in her tongue as well.

"Your soldiers burned our fields. Your soldiers burned our ships with our soldiers aboard. And now? The war's been over for three years, but there isn't anyone one to work the fields but children."

"I'm not proud of everything Borolia's done," I said, to be diplomatic. It was a true statement, but it wasn't what I really wanted to say. I wanted to point out that the war took its toll on us as well. The war claimed my mother when the navy's longguns struck the docks where she'd worked, my father when the munitions plant exploded. And Tar had wanted to conquer Borol as much as we'd wanted the reverse.

"That's good," she said. And for most of the day, neither of us spoke.

The second to last stop was the town of Halar, at the eastern edge of Vorronia, and the train pulled in shortly after sunset. The train car emptied, but filled just as quickly again with soldiers in imperial gold and green.

"They're done with their empire-sanctioned brawling and vandalism for the month and are returning to the front so that they can kill more foreigners," my seatmate informed me.

"Oh," I said.

"Why're you going to the front, then, foreigner? You a soldier?"

"No," I told her, "I'm a journalist."

9

"You're a whore, then," she said, "same as me. That's respectable."

I wanted to argue her point, but had a hard enough time formulating my reasoning in Boroli, let alone Vorronian. I said nothing.

I slept badly in my seat. The soldiers were boisterous and boring, with no interest in sleep at all. My seatmate snored softly, her head against the window, and I reclined as well as I could and waited for dawn.

The moon cast a pale glow on the landscape outside the window as we left the pastures and farmlands behind. The Gongol river tossed itself across rapids, the white foam spraying up towards the tracks that ran alongside the riverbed, and soon canyon walls raised up around us. I fell asleep at last, lulled to sleep by the rhythm of the train and the ethereal visage of the ice that encased the world around me.

....

Outpost 539 was unimpressive—though to be fair I was likely to be irritated by most anything by the time I arrived, bleary-eyed and grumpy, at the end of the line. We'd left the canyon lands behind us in the night, arriving in the foothills of the Cerracs and their attendant maple forests. A cluster of four stone buildings stood like gravestones in a fire-cleared field, the scorch marks still visible on the tree line, and a palisade of upturned logs did what it could to keep the wild at bay. The outpost's "train station" was a boardwalk and the only people waiting for us there were two military men.

One directed the outpour of soldiers, then departed with them. The other one was there for me.

"First Armsman Mitos Zalbii," he said, saluting.

"Dimos," I replied.

He stood at attention saluting for several awkward moments until I caught on.

"Dimos Horacki," I said, managing an amateur salute.

"We'll wait here for our carriage," Mitos said, and I took a seat on a bench on the platform. My seatmate from the train emerged a few moments later, elaborately made up and wearing a fine bustle that gave her body the S-curve that society demanded of women. No one met her, and she walked off on her own.

Mitos and I waited for another two hours. I had a thousand questions for him, but instead of asking them I dozed in and out of sleep. When our armored wagon arrived, drawn by six horses, I boarded it and slept some more.

Two

In a war between armies, like the Vorronian war that Borolia so recently won, the "front" is a dynamic, but tangible, geography. It exists. Though inadvisable, one can stand on it or cross it. Armies wait in barracks or trenches or repurposed city buildings and fire guns at one another like gentlemen (or gentlewomen in the Vorronian case, as that culture historically lacks the Borolian censure of women combatants).

But the new war was against territories and not nations, against peoples and not armies. The front in a war like that is amorphous, and from talking to soldiers, it's largely a state of mind. To be at the front means to be ready for battle.

At the time I was sent out, no one even knew the country of Hron existed. The Cerracs were just a territory to be conquered and colonized, with only a handful of villages and towns to speak of. The snow-capped mountains were just to be an eastern wall for the empire, butting up against Ora. The Imperial forces expected little resistance. Thankfully, they were wrong.

....

I woke up groggy as the carriage came to a halt, but my mood was a thousand times improved. Mitos was staring out the window, vaguely bored, at the leafless trees beyond.

"Hey," I asked, pretending I was startled. "Who're you? Where am I? What did I have to drink?"

Mitos replied with a short-lived, sardonic smile. "Glad you're awake, Mr. Horacki. I am to be your handler. We are in charge of one another, you and I. If I tell you what to do, you will obey me to the letter without question—I am responsible for your safety and frankly, you're at the front. So I'm in charge of you, but you're in charge of the story. You tell me what you need and I'll do my best to make it happen. Am I understood?"

"Yes," I said, sitting up on the bench.

"'Yes, sir,' you mean. You will call me 'sir,' Mr. Horacki," Mitos told me.

"Yes sir," I said. I'd probably never said "yes sir" before in my life, and I honestly didn't plan to make it a habit, but I saw no reason to make an issue of it.

....

The winter sun was warm on my face, but a mountain breeze found its way through my overcoat and I shivered as soon as I had both feet on the ground outside the carriage. The land smelled frozen and dead. Leafless aspens crowded in around me, and the Cerracs loomed close in on the horizon.

An honor guard of sorts was waiting for us: seven solemn men with horse and rifle, saluting Mitos and me. The gold and lime green of their dress uniform stood out strongly against the snow, rocks, and trees, marking them as targets from a mile away. Having just been told at some length about dangerous conditions at the front, I was not reassured.

"Take this," Mitos said, handing me a revolver in a gun belt. I had never touched a firearm in my life. On my second try, I buckled it on correctly. I then mounted a blue roan hack and we started out into a path among the trees, leaving the carriage and driver on the road.

After hardly a minute, all traces of respect fled our escort and they began to talk and laugh amongst themselves. "A hack on a hack," I heard one say. I'm all for puns, but it wasn't hard to realize that it wasn't well-intentioned. Most of the soldiers I met could scarcely abide my presence and made little secret of that fact.

I took out my pipe, packed it with tobacco, and began to smoke. It kept me relaxed. It was a strange afternoon, winding up that hillside. The world was silent and desolate and beautiful, but every time I let myself get caught up in that beauty, either some trace of disparaging conversation would drift to my ears or I'd find myself remembering that I was at the front in the company of men dressed in a startlingly inappropriate color scheme for their surroundings.

I offered Mitos my pipe, but he declined.

By the time we found our way to the soldiers' encampment, the gloaming was upon us and the scarce warmth of the sun fled from the world. The camp was a neat collection of tents and pavilions radiating out from a natural alcove in the cliff face. Cannon and other large guns faced outward from a palisade, and a bunker overlooked it all from atop the cliff.

General Armsman Dolan Wilder stood just inside the palisade to greet us. He wore his frock coat and his signature top hat, and was of course recognizable at a glance.

"Good day!" he called as we rode up.

The men accompanying me saluted and dismounted, then filed off to other duties. All but Mitos, who stayed at my side.

Wilder took the reins of my hack as I dismounted, and I followed him to a stable. The stablehand was a brute of a man with a shock of startlingly blonde hair who yanked at the reins and spit on the poor mare when she didn't respond graciously.

From there we walked down the central boulevard of camp, a muddy street paved with loose rocks and sticks. Cook fires were all around.

"In a good war," Wilder began, "a civilized war, a man may keep a cook fire at any point he likes. He is safe behind his own lines. But here, in the Cerracs, we fight savages. We cook in the twilight, when it's too dark to see smoke and too bright to see flame."

A soldier my father's age squatted in the mud, stirring a large pot. He looked at Wilder and saluted. Wilder saluted him in return.

"There are more than two hundred men in this camp," the General Armsman said. "And do you know what I fear the most?"

The question was rhetorical, and it was clear that he wasn't likely to care much for my personal opinions.

"The guerilla mindset is not a healthy one, you understand. It's a poison. I fight this war for His Majesty, above all else, but I also fight it for civilization. I fight for a world where we solve problems with metered justice and law, where men don't skulk about in forests. I fight savagery with savagery and I have no fear of death, my own or my men's. The only thing I fear is that we might become twisted by all this savagery, that we might fall ill with it."

Wilder led me to his command pavilion, distinguished from the tents around us only by its size and the four guards stationed around it. Once inside, a passable dinner of bird and root vegetables, as well as his five highest-ranking officers, awaited us. The General drank his liquor out of a snifter while the rest of the entourage drank theirs from clay mugs.

I was introduced to each man in turn, though the only name I can recall now is that of Lord Vasterly, the Major Armsman—third-in-command. Danis Lonel, Wilder's First Captain and second-in-command, was away. No matter as to the rest of these officers' names, however. They are dead to a man now, and I see no reason to celebrate their lives by ascribing them their names herein.

I took my seat at Wilder's side and took a pleasant sip of brandy. "What are we up against?" I asked, my first question to the man who was to be the subject of my writing.

"Bandits," he answered. "Simple bandits. I'm sure that before we came, these dirty outlaws were robbing homesteads and villages, but a few of them have turned their attentions and guns on us. And worse, a lot of these hovels are sheltering them. But we're here to bring the King's peace to the Cerracs, and a handful of half-starved criminals will be of little threat."

Then we ate. The officers had been waiting for our arrival, and they tore into the food with the sort of hunger I swear I only see in those who risk their lives on a day-to-day basis. As bones of our meal were scattered on our plates like dead foes, the banter began.

"Caught Greig and Halmos going at it in the forest today." Lord Vasterly sneered as he spoke, his heavy black mustache curling up with his lips. "Greig had his pants around his ankles, his arms around a tree. He was moaning like a girl."

"With a man today, with a goat tomorrow," another man suggested. A cliche in the army, I was soon to discover.

All the officers laughed at the joke. Wilder, for his part, smiled politely, knowingly.

"I'm not sure I understand," I said. It took me some time to word my question as safely as I could. "Is homosexuality looked down upon here?"

Their eyes and their silence were heavy on me. After a bit, Mitos answered me, surely more diplomatically than anyone else would have. "Not everything that passes as acceptable behavior among civilians is acceptable in the army."

Wilder spoke next, always looking for the chance to sound wise. "The Vorronian army allowed women in its ranks and proved beyond the slightest doubt that at least some women are every bit as competent in warfare as the average man. And yet His Majesty's army doesn't allow women to join. Why is that?"

He swirled his brandy about the snifter and answered his own question. "We don't allow women in His Majesty's army because their sexual availability destroys the social fabric we work so hard to maintain. Homosexual men make themselves available to other men and have the same effect."

I nodded. I even, bless my patriotic heart, tried to be understanding of someone arguing that men of my persuasion were not welcome. It didn't work, but I tried.

"We're in camp one more day," Mitos told me after the meal, "before we're off."

"Where're we going?" I asked.

"Elsewhere," he said. The man was inscrutable, as always.

The food was good, for winter rations, but it didn't sit well in my stomach owing to the company. And, later on my cot in my oilcloth tent, I slept badly.

The next morning, I rose with a clear head and a new determination. Whatever I saw, I was going to see as a journalist. I was there to observe and report. The truth, the bare facts, would vilify or heroize these soldiers, and I saw it as my duty to remain objective and detached. It was that determination, for better or worse, that saw me through much of my time at the front.

I rose from my cot, with its heavy wool blankets, and dressed in the freezing morning air. Mitos had left me a woolen civilian uniform—identical to those worn by the rest of the soldiers but completely devoid of demarkations—and it was warm and well-tailored. My cold hands fumbled as I tied my boots, but on the whole I didn't really mind the weather. In a way, the mountain winter was a refreshing change from the smog, humidity, and general miasma of the city I'd left behind. Everything felt crisp and sharp, and the air was fresh. The wind carried the smell of the forest into the camp.

There was no mirror, and I'd brought none with my shaving kit. I refused to fret about the situation, however—a few day's stubble has never done a man's face any harm.

I set out from my tent to find something to eat. I had met—and formed an opinion of—the officers, but the enlisted men were largely unknown to me.

"Hey journalist," a man cried, in a thick Vorronian accent, as I walked past, "why don't you eat with us?"

"We'll feed you if you write us up in the *Review*," his friend said.

They had pancakes and eggs, so I took up their offer. Both the men were young, younger than me, and might have been brothers. It can be hard to tell men in uniform apart, however, and I really only remember that both had ear-length shaggy black hair and the dark-olive Vorronian complexion and that one had a mole on his nose.

"So why'd you join the Army?" I asked, while they loaded up a tin dish with food.

"Whores," the one with the mole said.

"I want to kill somebody," the other one told me.

"Horseshit, both of you," I said, in Vorronian. "I'm not going to lie in the papers. Why'd you join the Army?"

They looked at one another and shrugged identical shrugs. Brothers or childhood best friends.

"Only job that will keep me fed," the one with the mole told me in Vorronian.

"Yeah," the other one said. "It's this or farming but my aunt says it's going to be a drought year and to be honest I never liked farming."

"And the whores though," the mole said. "And the killing. Those weren't lies. Only lie I've told in awhile is when I told the recruiter I was old enough to join."

The breakfast was good, and I thanked them for their time.

But they weren't the only ones who wanted me to write about them, though they were among the most polite. As I walked through camp unescorted, the soldiers did their best to cajole, harass, and even threaten me to grant them eternal fame by way of the written word. By instinct, I walked back to the stables, the only place I'd been in camp other than the command tent and my own quarters.

I heard the rhythmic pounding of hammer on steel and walked up to see a powerful, squat man in the process of shoeing a horse. He had a black and gray mane almost like a horse's, shaved on the sides, short on top and longer in the back—a haircut popular in the lower class areas of Vorronia, from what I knew.

I was watching him at his work for probably half a minute before he noticed me. He put in the final nail, set the horse's hoof on the ground, then turned to face me. He grinned, and I realized he'd gone partly gray quite young—he couldn't have been a day over thirty.

"Journalist!" he said. I was right—by the accent, he was from the lower class of Vorronia, probably from Tar.

"Not you too," I said, in Vorronian.

"Don't worry," he said, switching to his native tongue and clearly happy for it. "I don't want to be immortalized in print. Least of all for doing such despicable work as shoeing horses for the army."

This response surprised and endeared me immediately.

"No?" I asked.

He set down his tools and came to join me by the door. "No," he said. "There's no pride in this for me. At best, it's work—and who likes to work for other people?—and at worst I'm party to murder. To conquest. To the expansion of the same empire that so recently conquered Tar."

"Why do you do it?" I asked.

"I'll tell you, but you can't put me or what I say in your articles," he said. "Not yet. Not until I'm dead or free of this place."

"I swear," I said.

"Then I'm going to trust you. Don't betray that, my new friend, or you'll get me hanged. What's your name?"

"Dimos Horacki," I told him.

"A pleasure to meet you, Dimos," he said. "My name's Vinessay Solock. You can call me Vin."

He led me out away from the stable and towards the gate in the palisades. As we approached, the three pikemen on duty stood to attention, though they did not salute.

"Your business?" one asked.

"I intend to take our guest here, the journalist, to see the gibbet."

They looked at one another, considering his words, then the same man responded. "Very well."

"Formalities," he said as we walked out the gate, "are either a sign of the love and worship to be found in ceremony and ritual, or more often, they're the sign of a weak mind desperately clinging to power and law in the face of the wilds, of chaos."

"Just who are you?" I asked. I was starting to get nervous. I had no idea what to make of the man, and for a moment I worried he might be a Vorronian nationalist, on a mission of sabotage. I shivered, half with fear, half with excitement.

"I'm a farrier," he said. "Nothing more. My mother was a strong woman, though, and I like to think she left me a lot. She died in the war before the war, when I was a baby."

I'd heard the term before, somewhere in my research, and I wracked my brain to place it. "The revolution?" I asked. Before the war against Vorronia had broken out, there'd been an uprising by a mix of anarchists and republicans. Borolia had ridden in to the rescue, only to grab territory in the north of the country as soon as the peasants were put down with gunfire. That treachery had sparked the war, not the longgun strike on the Borol harbor, despite what we print in the *Borol Review*.

Not ten feet from the front gate, we took a path that took us alongside the palisades and, two minutes later, to the gallows. A strong oak beam projected out from the top of the wall, supporting the weight of two hanged men. Each had the same haircut as Vin.

"They look like you," I said.

"They *are* like me," he responded. "Conscripts. Caught deserting."

I looked in horror at the rotten flesh that hung loose on the prisoners' bones, then turned to Vin. He was smiling, a tight, sad smile.

"As sad as I am, looking at two of my friends hanging from a beam in the Cerracs, I know that there were four more with them that left that night. I wish I'd had the courage to join them. The four that escaped, or even these two here. I don't like this work, and I don't know if I like these mountains. I don't like my company, and least of all do I like myself."

Three

The next morning, with the sun still below the mountain, I rode out with Wilder, Mitos, and seventy men. We picked our way down the trail to the road, single- and double-file. I rode with Wilder near the front, though he was quiet that morning. Once we reached the road, the General galloped off ahead with the vanguard.

Roads in the Cerracs are a lot like the roads in the north of Borolia: packed dirt and gravel with deep wagon ruts. The main force of the army rode at a walk, to keep pace with the supply and ammunition wagons, and I had plenty of time to stare at, and make note of, the magnificent forests and hills around me. But my hopes for quiet contemplation were quickly dashed—an army, as it turns out, even a small one, doesn't go anywhere quietly. The wagons rumbled and clanked, and the men shouted and boasted. They fired their guns into the forest at the slightest noise, shooting at squirrels and bears and wild turkeys or just the sounds of the wind.

Most of the time, roads in the mountains follow the course of rivers, and that morning's ride was no exception. "What river is that?" I asked Mitos.

He shrugged.

I asked the man to my left, a gray-haired veteran.

"A wet one," he said.

I gave up on questioning the men after that.

Some time later, we found Dolan Wilder and his vanguard waiting for fresh horses. Wilder's horse was dead, ridden to death by the man who wore spurs as sharp as a barber's razor. Wilder mounted a spare gelding and fell in beside me.

Not long after, we reached the village of Steknadi. I only learned its name a month later; his Majesty's Army didn't know or care who these people were, let alone what they chose to name their settlements. On Wilder's map, they were numbered instead of named.

"They must have seen us coming," Wilder told me. A hundred or so villagers were gathered on a cobbled square in the center of town, surrounded by their goats and mountain ostriches and gigantic shepherd dogs. The peasants were unarmed and clearly afraid.

"If it weren't for that sow of a horse," he told me, as though in confidence, "we'd have been on them before they'd had a chance to disguise themselves and take off with the weaponry."

The unit spread out over the village, securing the road and the most visible paths into the forest, while Lord Vasterly rode in to speak with the assembled peasants.

"I'd like to hear what he has to say," I told Mitos.

"It seems peaceful enough here," my handler granted, and the two of us rode closer.

"You're in the Empire now," Vasterly was saying. His Cer—the dialect of Vorronian spoken in the mountains—was terrible, accented so thickly I doubt more than half the crowd understood him. "You'll be under our watch. Under the King's watch. We give you peace."

Everything was silent. Even the wind was still. Even the goats did not bleat, the ostriches did not call out.

"What peace is that, fat man?" a boy from the crowd finally asked. "The peace of the grave?"

Vasterly drew his gun and aimed it at the boy. "If you so please," he answered.

"The King's peace," Wilder interrupted, riding up alongside Vasterly and me. His Cer, while accented, was a thousand times more studied than Vasterly's. "We extend mercy and justice to his citizens and reserve our bullets—" at this he took a moment to stare down his subordinate, "for his enemies. Your enemies."

"We have to set an example," Lord Vasterly said, in Boroli.

"We just did," Wilder replied. "And you will not interrupt me in any language."

"Yes sir."

Vasterly began to explain the terms of the village's new governance. Largely, it consisted of taxation—to be taken that very day—of herd animals and food stockpiles. This news apparently didn't come as a surprise, though it was clearly unwelcome.

Three soldiers approached, dragging a struggling woman. The smallest of the men stepped forward to address Wilder.

"We found her trying to get into the woods," the man said. His voice was soft, his eyes were bright.

"I had to find my herd," she said, in formal Vorronian.

"What she say?" one of her handlers asked, in the thickest northern drawl I'd ever imagined.

"Said she had to find her herd," the soft-voiced man answered.

"Arhuh huh huh," the man laughed. "She had what to go crawling if she was looking for ostriches? Maybe what they was tiny little ones?"

Wilder drew his crop and struck the man across the face, then the back. "You will not speak in such a peasant tongue in His Majesty's army."

"Yes sir," the man said, trying and failing to master his accent.

The man in the top hat turned to the woman and spoke in her language. "You were off to warn the rebels, no?"

"Fuck you," she said, in Boroli.

Dolan Wilder dismounted and led the party of us—the woman, her three attendants, myself, and my attendant—into the forest for nearly two miles. He spoke to her at length in Cer, telling her what a merciful man he could be. She refused to speak.

At length, Wilder gave up and ordered her tied to a tree to be "salted."

The soft-voiced man obliged with a smile, securing her with rope to the trunk of the ancient aspen. He unsheathed his bayonet, cut open the woman's flank, and sprinkled powder into the wound. She began to howl in pain immediately.

We left her there and walked back.

"What was that?" I asked Wilder. But he didn't answer. His face was a mask, his eyes expressionless.

"What was that?" I asked Mitos.

"Gorsalt," he answered. "Hallucinogenic salt from Ora. It induces nightmares and attracts wolves."

"Why'd you do it?" I asked the soft-voiced stranger.

"Wasn't me, not really," he told me. "It was an order. Wilder's the one who gave it."

But it wasn't Wilder's bayonet that cut into the woman's flesh.

It was not by his hands that she was salted. It is in this way that the Imperial Army—indeed, any authoritarian military force—eschews individual responsibility. If there is a devil in this world, it does its work through hierarchy.

....

We rode from Steknadi to a nearby lake and set up camp for the night. Wilder was in a sour mood and took his dinner alone, so I walked out to the rocky beach. My greatcoat took the sting from the air and the moon above was gibbous and lovely.

I thought about the salting, and fear began its way to the fore of my brain. I couldn't tell why I'd been invited along to witness the woman's execution. Maybe Wilder had meant to scare me, but honestly, I thought it then and I think it now, I just think the man saw ruthlessness as a virtue. Wilder wasn't trying to scare *me* because I wasn't even a person to him, I was a vessel through which he could communicate with the world. I was an object, a tool. I was a journalist. Wilder wasn't trying to scare *me*, he was trying to scare the world.

Tobacco wasn't enough to calm me down, though I smoked quite a bit that evening. First conscription, now this. My loyalty was shaking, and I didn't know what to make of that.

My friends and I in Borol used to talk in the bars about ourselves as cynical patriots—we knew what was wrong with Borolia, or so we thought, but we were pretty glad when our side won the war. We hated the rich and maybe we didn't agree with everything the King said or did, but we loved our soldiers almost enough to sign up ourselves.

The stars my witness, that evening at the lake in the Cerrac mountains, I decided it was my job as a writer, maybe even my duty to my country, to tell the truth about my time at the front. No matter if it angered a man so civil and terrifying as Dolan Wilder. I'm not sure what I would have done, however, if I'd known just what effect my vow would have on my safety.

....

I was solemn the next day's ride. I tried writing on horseback—a terrible and illegible failure, that—before giving up on getting much more done than thinking in the saddle. And I'd started to grow bored of just thinking.

"Hey Mitos," I asked.

He rode up closer.

"I'm trying to write about what's been going on, and I don't have the words for everything. Those shirts, or dresses, or whatever they are that the peasants wear. What are they called?" Everywhere we'd been, the residents wore basically the same garb: woolen pants tucked into boots, with some sort of long shirt that came down to mid-thigh, and a bright, woven cloak over it all.

"I don't know," he said. "Shirts? Maybe a tunic? How does it matter?"

"Hey, Mr. Journalist," someone called out. I turned and saw a soldier, my age with long black hair, riding a black horse. He rode up on my left.

"I just put it together. You're Horacki, right?"

"Yeah," I said.

"You wrote that article! You're the one who got the Grinder burned down!"

I hadn't been recognized on the street in four years. My hand went into my satchel, wrapped around my brass knuckles.

"I'm glad you did, is all," the soldier said. "I grew up there. I hated that place. So thanks." He gave a salute, then spurred his horse up to the front of the ranks. My hand relaxed.

"What was that about?" Mitos asked.

"You didn't hear about it? An article I wrote, maybe four years ago."

"I've been in Vorronia for ten," Mitos told me.

"My first big story. I'd been at the *Review* a year and finally got the go-ahead. After my folks died in the war, I got sent to Miss Grinosti's Boarding House. We called it, and her, the Grinder. I was barely a teenager and was a ward of the state. Ran away a couple times, always ended up back there. After I got out..."

"After you got out, you swore you'd see the place destroyed," Mitos said.

"No, no, nothing like that. Well, okay, that's close. After I got out I swore I'd tell the world what I'd been through. I'd show just how terrible that place was. Miss Grinosti worked us hard, didn't teach us a thing. We barely got fed. The ceiling leaked, our bathwater was red with rust. Disease went rampant. So I wrote about it. As a journalist. I did my research—I found the bribed inspectors, the forged forms, the overseas customers. But, well, when the article ran, Miss Grinosti set herself and the boarding house on fire. Three kids died."

"How'd you feel about that?" Mitos asked. He was staring straight ahead, poorly concealing anger.

"Awful," I said.

"Good," he said. "You murdered four people."

"That's not quite fair," I said.

"By the King it *is* fair," he said. "That woman didn't teach you a thing? No? Then how'd you walk out of there at 17 and get hired by the best paper in Borol? And you think your life was hard because the *ceiling leaked*? While you were living for free I was fighting a war."

"It was my father taught me to write," I said. There wasn't much to say, after that. I'd felt guilty for years after the article ran, but I hadn't murdered anyone. That was on Miss Grinosti, that was on the bribed inspectors and the whole system that let that place be the Grinder. I didn't feel guilty for exposing it, I felt guilty because my plan hadn't worked—I'd wanted to see the place fixed up, not destroyed.

....

Two days later we razed the village of Sotoris to the ground. Three score wooden buildings were put to the torch, houses and halls and granaries and stables. Three people—a woman, her husband, and their twelve-year-old child—had had the temerity to meet us as enemies instead of liberators, had shot at us from the second floor window of their three-hundred-year-old house. Their bullets missed the soldiers, but one of them managed to wound a horse before a score of armed men captured the family alive.

I say it was "we" who razed Sotoris because I consider myself complicit, I say it was "we" because I did nothing to stop them. Because I saw myself as a journalist, impartial. Because I thought honest words alone would raise me up and out of sin. Because I was wrong. It's possible I will forgive myself eventually, but it's not likely.

The child was executed immediately, garroted in a chair in the center of town before the assembled villagers. It seemed monstrous at first, but truly it was a mercy. The woman was taken off by Vasterly for interrogation while her husband was tied to the chair on top of his dead child.

"Flinders under his nails, if you would," Wilder commanded to the soft-voiced man. The man ran his knife along the chair, carving off long splinters. There was no hesitation, no savoring of the bound man's pain. The torturer just removed the husband's boots and, quickly and efficiently, rammed the wood under his toenails.

The man screamed, and someone in the crowd shouted out.

"Execute the unruly," Wilder commanded, and a trio of soldiers strode into the crowd, found the shouter, and cut his throat.

"Pull out the flinders," Wilder commanded, and the soft-voiced man obliged.

"Where are the rebels?" Wilder asked.

"I wouldn't tell you if I knew," the tortured man replied.

Wilder removed his sidearm and shot the man down through the top of his skull. I think he did it that way so that the bullet wouldn't pass through and hurt anyone in the crowd. Maybe he did it to minimize the blood.

Lord Vasterly returned shortly, pulling his black riding gloves back on, and took Wilder aside to confer. I couldn't overhear, but after they spoke, Wilder pistol-whipped his third-in-command, bloodying the man's temple.

"Raze the village," Wilder said. "But hurt no one else."

The villagers were too cowed to do more than mutter protestations and cry loudly in sorrow while everything they owned, everything they had built with their own hands or inherited from their families, was destroyed by uniformed strangers. I stood there, observing, trying to maintain a journalistic detachment, as an unspeakable cruelty was levied upon the people of the Cerrac mountains. We taxed them of almost their entire herd and then left them, homeless and helpless, in the dead of winter.

....

With the fire still raging behind us, we started back to camp. Mitos was ever at my side.

"Why did he hit Vasterly?" I asked my handler.

"Wilder's a gentleman," he replied, "and he doesn't tolerate officers who disrespect His Majesty's fairer subjects, even those who don't want to *be* His Majesty's subjects. Lord Vasterly has been demoted to Second Armsman, and he will be lucky if he holds onto his lordship when he returns from this campaign."

"And this village, weren't those His Majesty's houses and halls we just burned?"

I heard the clip clop of hooves while Mitos took his time formulating an answer. "Wilder is an eloquent man, but it's his penchant for irrational violence that commands authority, not his speeches. That's true of his troops and that's true of his new subjects. The Empire offers a lot to the Cerracs. The roads and the trade will come, eventually, but they're going to be laid on a bed of respect and submission."

We rode in silence for the rest of the evening, and when we camped in a field, Wilder took his meal alone once more. I stayed up late into the night composing my first column, which I handed to the mail carrier in the morning. I stuck to the objective truth, which was nearly my undoing.

Four

It was less than four hours after we returned to camp when Wilder called me into his tent. A brazier tried and failed to light the corners the sun couldn't reach, and a uniformed stranger stood warming his hands over the flame. The man was short and thin, with a close-cropped red beard and wire-rimmed spectacles. Despite his officer's regalia, he didn't strike me as soldierly.

"Mr. Horacki, I would like you to meet First Captain Danis Lonel, my second-in-command," Wilder said, by way of introducing me to the stranger.

"Danis, please," the man said.

I liked him instantly, a fact that caught me by surprise.

"Lonel made First Captain in the Vorronian War," Wilder went on, "and I served under him. A fine man, and an excellent scout."

Danis smiled at this. I couldn't tell if his smile was genuine or sardonic. To this day I sometimes wonder—he was an intriguing man.

"We've had reports of raiders to the southeast harassing a Vorronian settler. Stole some cattle. Tomorrow, First Captain Lonel will take you and a dozen men to find the bandits. You will engage and capture or kill them."

"I don't believe a dozen men can do it," Lonel replied. "Give me fifty. And no offense to this man, but a tactical raid is no place for a civilian."

Dolan turned his gaze on me and smiled. "Lonel made First Captain in Vorronia. And here, three years later, he's First Captain still. He's a... cautious man. Cautious men have their place in a command structure but that place is *not* the top."

Dolan looked back to Lonel. "You'll take a dozen men and find these bandits. If at all possible, you are to engage them. If that's not possible, you are to return here with information. And you will bring the journalist. Mitos will see to his safety."

"I'd been hoping to have a chance to see camp—" I began.

"You'll leave in the morning. The last man you spoke to in camp, the farrier, has deserted. I don't know what you told him, I don't know what lies he told you. You're not here to speak with the enlisted men here at camp: you are here to write a story on this campaign and the officers who run it. That is an order. You might think that you, a civilian, aren't required to obey orders, but if so, you're wrong. You're a servant of the Sovereign, and I represent your Sovereign's will. You're dismissed."

I nodded and turned to leave. Out of the corner of my eye, sitting on Wilder's desk, I saw the green envelope that contained my first column, the one I had sent out with the day's mail immediately upon my return to camp.

....

Even in the company of Danis Lonel, I spent my days riding in silence. Mitos had long since stopped talking to me except as necessary, as neither of us liked the other, and Danis was friendly enough but seemed to have little to say.

I grew to begrudge the isolation. Had I been alone, I would likely have spent my time observing the birds, the clouds, the frost-bit grasses that peaked out from the side of the road. Instead, I was surrounded by men who spoke to one another all day but who could scarcely spare a cigarette, let alone a word, for me.

"If we're scouts in hostile terrain," I asked Danis one evening as we ate, "why're we out here riding in broad daylight?"

"These are our mountains," the officer replied, drinking brandy from his steel canteen. "We can't be seen skulking around in the darkness like common thieves."

The military mind of the Imperial officer is beyond me.

On the seventh day, we reached a tiny homestead of herders and levied a tax. We were greeted politely, as welcome conquerers, before riding away a short time later. My belly was full of good meat and fresh fruit and the sun was out, breaking through the shade of the maples and dappling the ancient road before us. A herd of taxed ostriches and goats kept pace. Danis looked to me, his pipe hanging out of the corner of his mouth, his hands on the reins.

He opened up to me, for the first time. But I think he spoke of all the things one would like to see written about in print—his love of country, of his hometown Winne, how much he missed his wife and family, those sorts of things.

"I used to think," he said to me, after awhile, "that if anyone came into Winne and tried this, we'd kill them for it. But that's just the thing, isn't it? Someone already did. It was just a long, long time ago. That's why we have Borolia."

That was the smartest thing he ever said to me. And to this day

I can't figure out why he said it with such a smile on his face. Or really, why he told me that at all. But unfortunately for my curiosity—and fortunately for the people living the in Cerrac mountains—his pondering was interrupted by gunfire and the men around us died reaching for their guns. The ostriches began to stampede through the horses, off into the trees.

I've been in a few firefights now, which I can't really recommend, and time does some strange things when there are bullets involved. The first volley was over before it had started, but afterwards I felt like I had all the time in the world to drop from my saddle and into the dust. Maybe I should have pulled my gun and shot back, but it honestly didn't occur to me to do so.

The Imperial Army lost that fight before the enemy even showed itself. There were fourteen of us riding that day, and ten were wounded or killed in the first volley.

To his credit, Mitos Zalbii, with whom I had shared as few words as possible, stood over me and died with a rifle in his hands. I never liked him, and he never liked me, but he died fulfilling the duty he had been arbitrarily assigned. That duty being my wellbeing, I still think of him fondly and genuinely mourn his passing.

When Mitos fell forward, half his face torn off by a fusillade of rifle fire, I looked up and saw Danis with his hands above his head, his pistol and saber still untouched at his side.

"I give up!" he shouted in Cer.

Five

About a score of brigands came into view, on foot, from the hill to our right, the woods to our left, and the road before us. Each bore a pistol or rifle, and they were roughly equally men and women of a mix of ethnicities, though largely Cer. All of them wore balaclavas, scarves, or other masks over their faces.

The bandits walked through the mess and shot the wounded men and horses. One woman and two men, one short and olive skinned, the other tall with a Borolian's fair complexion, approached Danis and me, guns drawn.

I stood slowly, raising my heads above my head.

"I am the officer here," Danis said. "I surrender."

"Yes," the shorter man said, then shot the First Captain in the face.

I entirely disassociated at this point. I saw what was happening around me, but my body shut down to keep panic at bay. When the woman walked towards me, gun held limp at her side, I was certain I was going to die.

"I know you," she said, in Vorronian.

"The train," I answered.

"You're that whore of a journalist."

I probably nodded. At least, I wanted to nod, and I might have succeeded.

"If you want," she said, "you can come with us."

I think I nodded again.

The brigands took their time going over the site of the ambush, strangely playful and laughing as they went. They took the guns and the horses. They stripped each dead man naked and took their uniforms.

One very young woman, rifling through Danis's saddlebags, stood up and shouted. "I found a map!" She unfolded the canvas and several of her compatriots came over to look before returning to their own looting.

The man who killed Danis Lonel stood by me the entire time. The first thing he did was politely relieve me of my gun belt. He checked the revolver, saw it was loaded, and strapped the belt around his waist. He then slung his rifle over his back and waited and watched. He stayed calm, never acted aggressively towards me, never pointed a weapon at me. If he and his friends hadn't just killed every person I knew within a half a hundred miles, I might have even relaxed.

I was a journalist, I told myself. If I survived, I'd better have something to write about. I tried to keep track of the details I would use later. I can't say this calmed me down, but it kept me from entirely falling apart. So I stayed detached and kept stock of what happened around me.

The bandits were dressed roughly the same as the peasants I'd seen in the mountains: wool pants; a long, dress-like shirt, and a thick winter cloak. But where those in villages had preferred woven patterns of reds and blues and purple, the bandits were dressed to match their surroundings: white, brown, and green.

My handler was a handsome man and kept looking at me. His green eyes looked out over the bandanna, his flat-top bowler was pulled low to hide much of his brow, but I could see emotion there. The man uncorked a ceramic flask of water, pulling up his mask past a neat-trimmed black beard to drink.

After a half an hour, a pair of brigands came out from the forest onto the road, accompanied by the greater part of the lost flock of ostriches and two massive Cerrac Shepherds. I'd seen a few of these dogs over the past few weeks, but they were still a little unnerving—a Cerrac Shepherd is almost half my height at the shoulder and is easily sixty pounds heavier than me. They're covered in thick fur and have the cutest canine face you'll ever see, but they were originally bred to hunt bears before they were adapted to ostrich-herding duty. Imperial soldiers had an unfortunate tendency to shoot them at the slightest provocation, so I'd never met one up close.

An hour after the attack, all the brigands met back up to talk in the middle of the road, having loaded all of His Majesty's horses with the bounty of the kill. My handler stayed with me, just out of earshot from the impromptu meeting.

"What're you going to do with the bodies?" I asked, in Cer.

"Leave them for the vultures and wolves," he answered.

"Isn't that a bit... I don't know the word in Cer. Cold?"

The man took another pull from his flask. "I suppose it is," he said. "Do you feel like burying them?"

"No," I admitted.

"Neither do I," the man told me.

"We go!" the woman from the train shouted over to us.

"I hate to say this," the man said, "but if you're coming with us, we'll have to put a bag over your head for awhile."

....

I spent the ride condemning myself for how little I seemed to care about the scene I had witnessed. In retrospect, of course, I know that traumatizing events can take time to sink in, but for that long afternoon on horseback with nothing to see but a canvas sack and the hints of sun through the threads, I couldn't decide if my callousness meant I was a monster or just a damn good war correspondent.

I was mounted behind my handler on my own horse, and the bandit's rifle banged into my chest whenever I slumped forward too much. I caught snatches of conversation.

"Who is he?" one woman asked.

"The General met him on a train," my handler told her.

"Why's he alive?" she asked.

"He's a journalist," he answered.

She laughed. "That doesn't really answer the question."

"He didn't even draw his gun. I'm not going to kill a man who isn't a soldier."

"I could do it," she said, "if you like."

"No," my handler said.

We rode in silence awhile longer before another horse fell into step beside ours.

"He's a journalist? From Borolia?" a deep voice asked.

"Yes," I answered.

"How long were you with the soldiers?"

"Two weeks," I said.

"Glad you brought him," the man said. "He'll be useful."

There was something ominous in the way that the man said the word "useful," and for the first time, a real, deep fear made its way up my spine and into my brain. All I could do was keep breathing—deep breaths, down in my lower lungs. I told myself I was a journalist, that I was uninvolved. It worked, sort of.

....

I heard the waterfall from what must have been a quarter mile away, and by the time we reached it, I could hear little but the rush of crashing water.

We stopped, and my handler dismounted.

"You can take the hood off, now, if you'd like," he said, and I did.

The waterfall was something from a fairytale, dropping a hundred feet down the cliffside we stood atop to the canyon river below. Ice caked the walls around it, and the low sun made the frozen rocks sparkle and shine.

Overlooking the canyon, we stood at the very edge of an alpine meadow where horses—mountain ponies but for a few lowland thoroughbreds—ran unbridled and ostriches and goats wandered freely. A few shepherds, human and canine together, kept an eye on everything.

"My name is Sorros Ralm," my handler said. "And it's my pleasure to introduce you to the Free Company of the Mountain Heather."

"Dimos Horacki," I said. I offered my hand, which he took and clasped instead of shaking.

The men and women dismounting didn't look like it was in fact a pleasure to be meeting me, however. Not a one of them had removed their masks, and while none pointed weapons at me, many kept them slack in hand at their sides.

"We leave the livestock here, with some shepherds," Sorros explained, "and we'll make the rest of our trip on foot."

One or two at a time, all the bandits walked to the edge of the cliff and hopped down to a ledge below. The way would have been invisible if one didn't know where to look for it. I followed.

We started towards the waterfall, and the company struck up a song. They have asked me since to not put any of their lyrics or melodies into writing, and I will honor that wish, but know that it was a song of immense beauty, of hopeful words. A song of spring and war. There were numerous harmonies, and while not every person of the company was up to the task of holding a tune perfectly, it worked out all the same.

"The song is our passcode," Sorros informed me, during a break in the baritone part he had been singing. And not one hundred yards later, the ledge widened and we walked between two gun placements. The sentries on duty looked at us, counted, and grinned. It only then occurred to me that the bandits had killed thirteen soldiers without suffering a single casualty.

After the gun placement, the ledge widened, and around the next bend I saw a rather well-concealed guerilla camp: shacks and tents were pitched under the overhang of the cliff or in the shade of the low grove of bristlecone pines. It would be all but invisible to anyone atop the cliff.

The waterfall rushed right past, and my eye went immediately to the clever open-top pipe system they had erected to bring running water to their camp. His Majesty's army, for comparison, had made do with water bearers who carried jug after jug from a nearby stream.

Most of the Free Company left for various tasks around the camp, but Sorros, a few strangers, and the woman from the train they called the General stood around to ask me questions.

"Who are you?" Sorros asked. "And not your name. But who are you."

"I work for the *Borol Review*," I told them, "it's a paper. I'm on assignment to write about the war effort. They wanted me to write about Dolan Wilder."

"What do you know about him?" Sorros asked. "What does he eat, what does he drink? Where and when does he sleep? How does he treat his soldiers?"

I was terrified, but I didn't want to answer. So I asked a question. "You're not just bandits, are you?"

"Bandits?!" Sorros asked. "Mr. Wilder is the bandit. We're here in the mountains in the dead of winter because Borolian bandits have been harassing villages all along the edge of Hron. We're the militia."

"Hron?" I asked.

"Wilder," the General cut in. She'd taken off her mask. "Tell us about Wilder."

I looked at her, at the armed women and men around her, and it occurred to me that Sorros was likely telling the truth, that I might have been on the wrong side of this fight. I sighed, and my breath came out heavy and visible in the air in front of me.

"I won't," I said.

Someone cocked a gun. I couldn't see it, but I heard it. The General raised her hand to stop whomever it had been. I heard the gun uncock.

"You'll tell the whole goddamned world about him in an article but you won't tell us?" the General asked.

"Yeah," I said. "It's different and you know it."

"Write about us instead?" Sorros asked.

"What?" The question took me off guard. It took almost

everyone else off guard too, it looked like, because soon it was only myself, Sorros, and the General.

"I'm not going to kill you. You can stay here for awhile or you can leave. And if you're going to keep writing about the front, why don't you write about us? Get, you know, both sides of the story."

"Alright," I said. I couldn't imagine *not* writing about my experience in the hands of Borol's enemy.

Sorros grinned. I couldn't remember the last time I'd seen such an enthusiastic smile. He then turned to the General, took her hand in his, and stood on his toes to whisper in her ear. She started laughing, then kissed him on the mouth.

"I'm Nola," she said, offering her free hand to me.

"General Nola?" I asked.

"Not a chance," she said. "Don't listen to anyone who tells you otherwise."

After that, Nola walked off and Sorros took me to a well-built one-room shack set against the cliffside. The first two feet of the wall were unmortared stone, the rest of rough-hewn wood. Inside, it was decorated and insulated with heavy draped fabric in drab earth tones. There was no furniture save a wide sleeping mat against the center of the back wall. On the wall above it was a tapestry that radiated color into the otherwise dull quarters and depicted a forest scene of wild horses. In the lower left corner was a small crest I'd never seen before, of a horse with two horns, a bizarre mix of rhinoceros and unicorn.

"Is this place yours?" I asked my captor or host, whichever he was.

"I built it, and I've been staying here," he replied.

"You don't own it, is that the idea? It belongs to the Free Company?"

"I don't think we talk about things in the same way as you do. I think if I used possessive words around you, you'd get the wrong idea," he said. "At home, in Hronople, I 'owned' my home. I knew I'd be gone for so long, though, that I gave it away. Out here, we're at war, and a soldier of Hron doesn't 'own' much at all. I built this place, and I can make use of it, but I'd be a damned fool to not make use of it in the way that best serves us in this conflict. Anyone can come and go at any time, and I trust them not to invade my privacy without some reason."

"But you could bar them from doing so?"

"Why would I do that?" he asked. "If my heart wasn't with my people, would I be out here in the snow hunting soldiers?"

"Why *are* you here?" I asked.

"Your journalist questions will have to wait," he replied. "I'm going to go eat. You wouldn't be welcome to join us, I'm afraid, but Nola and I will be back soon and I'll bring you back a bowl of something."

"Am I free to go?"

"You have the queerest questions. I'm not detaining you here against your will. You're 'free to go.' You're free to wander the frozen mountains, lost, until you're eaten by wolves, if that's what you want to do."

He smiled as he said this, and I realized that he just thought I was a very, very strange man. At the time, I could scarcely understand his logic, however.

Sorros left me to my thoughts. I had so many it was hard to piece through them all. What did they really want with me? Why did they want me to write about them? Were they telling me the truth? Those thoughts were useless... the Free Company didn't seem to offer me harm, so a risky escape seemed like a poor option and whatever was going to happen was going to happen. Why had Wilder sent only fourteen of us out to attack the bandits? What was he doing with my column on his desk? Those were the more interesting questions. I lay back on the sleeping mat to think them through.

I woke with a start in the darkness when Sorros and Nola returned. Sorros had a huge wooden bowl that smelled of beets and set it before me, along with a wooden spoon.

"It's not very hot anymore," he said, by way of apology. "We stayed up late talking."

"We'll be gone most of the next two weeks," Nola told me.

"And, well, there's a chance we won't be coming back at all," Sorros said. "If we don't, then you can either make your way back to Vorronia—follow the river, it eventually joins up with the Gongol and will take you to the coast—or wait until spring when reinforcements are due. You can eat our stores, and if we don't return, start into the ostriches up above. I'm not sure how you'll be received by our replacements, to be honest."

"Where are you going?" I asked, though I was pretty sure I knew the answer.

"Desil found a map on one of your horses that includes the location of Wilder's camp. We're from these mountains—we think we can take them."

"There are hundreds of soldiers there at any time," I protested.

"We know the terrain," Nola said. "They won't see us coming. We'll hit them while they sleep and be gone before they wake. Maybe we won't get them all, but maybe we will."

I nodded. There was no way I was going to change their minds, and I wasn't even sure why I would want to. Only these two had shown me even a basic level of kindness. Why should I have cared what happened to their company?

Sorros took my hand in his warmly. "Goodbye, Dimos Horacki. If we don't return, I hope you survive and that you write about us honestly."

Nola smiled at me, then the two left me in the cabin. Off to follow the map to the camp. The map that Danis had had on his person. For some reason. It clicked together in my head—the map, my newspaper column, the small scouting party. I'd been sent off to die. Danis had been sent off to die. We'd been bait.

I stood up, spilling my still-untouched soup on the sleeping mat, and bolted out the door.

"Wait!" I shouted at the massed silhouettes who were just beginning to walk out of camp. Several turned and pointed rifles at me. Sorros, however, approached.

"It's a trap," I explained.

"You were part of it!" a voice shouted from the crowd. Crowds are good places from which to shout anonymous accusations.

"Not on purpose," I replied, then told them what I knew. Which, to be honest, wasn't that much.

"*This* could be the trap," another voice said, more calmly than the last.

"I suppose," I said, "though it wouldn't make too much sense."

"Why are you telling us?" someone asked.

"Did you miss the part where Wilder sent him off to die?" Nola asked.

Another woman, a stranger, nodded. "I believe him. At least enough to hear him out."

"There's an outcropping overlooking the camp. If I was Wilder, I'd have moved most of my troops up top, leaving only a skeleton crew down below. When you attack, they'll drop the mountain on you, or at least rain mortar."

"And kill their own troops?" asked a voice.

"Of course they'd kill their own troops," said another.

"If he's right," Nola said, "we can catch them on the overlook. Drive them to the edge and over. If he's wrong, we don't really lose anything."

"If he's wrong," Sorros said, "we'll lose the element of surprise."

"It's worth the risk," a voice said. "We should try it."

"All agreed?" a voice asked. "That we try this journalist's plan?"

"Aye," the crowd responded.

"Amendment," one voice replied. "We bring him with us. If he's lying, we shoot him in both legs and throw him off the cliff."

"Objection," another voice responded. "We bring him with us, and if he's lying, we kill him. But we do it as cleanly and quickly as circumstances allow."

My head was spinning trying to follow the conversation.

"Conceded," said the voice that had offered the amendment.

"Amendment," Nola offered. "If he's telling the truth, we give him a gun. They tried to kill him, afterall."

"All agreed?" a voice asked.

"Aye," the crowd responded.

I think that had he been from another culture, Sorros would have slapped me on the back. Instead, he just grinned.

Six

The way back to Wilder's camp was lit by a waning half-moon—unlike conquerors, the actual residents of the mountains felt no need to ride during daylight. I rode alone on a mountain pony while most of the rest of us went double on horses, and almost two dozen Cerrac Shepherds padded silently alongside. Our moon-shadows stretched far in front of us, and in that company I felt powerful.

Nola and Sorros shared a black thoroughbred mare and I most often rode alongside them, though sometimes I lagged back for a bit of solace. We spent a week on the march, camping during the day in caves or dark thickets. We skirted towns, afraid our presence might provide an excuse for reprisal. Our scouts, however, visited settlements almost every day and returned laden with provisions. One day, while eating mountain blackberry jam spread over fresh bread, I realized that food given freely tasted objectively better than food taken by force.

"The way you make decisions," I asked Sorros over dinner one morning. "Is no one in charge?"

"You're learning," Sorros said. "Yes, no one is in charge. We're all here because we want to be—or because we feel like we need to be—and we're all risking our lives. Why would it be appropriate for one person to tell me how it is I'm going to end my life? Shouldn't that be my own decision?"

"How do you get anything done?" I asked. I wasn't ready to tackle the ethical argument he presented, because I had never considered it before.

"You've seen it," he answered. "We listen to one another and discuss things. In council at home, decisions with a lot of people take awhile. Here in the Free Company, we try to speed things up a bit."

I nodded, but I didn't really understand.

....

While none of the Free Company was initially friendly with me, I had days to observe them and I started to distinguish between them. They became individuals instead of just a mass of nervous, armed strangers—which, to be fair, they also were. By the look of them, they were mostly in their early twenties like myself, though there were several among them with gray or white hair. The oldest was a woman most likely in her sixties. Most people respected her, but were maybe a bit afraid of her too. She was quiet most of the time, yet when she spoke people listened. The rest of the elders rode together, but she rode alone, at the front, her shotgun never far from her hand.

Then there was a group of five youths that stuck together every hour of the day. The youngest couldn't have been sixteen, the oldest might convince me she was twenty if she swore on her life. Everything was a game to them. During the day, they sat around camp and told stories and inside jokes. At night, they rode ahead or lingered behind, and they declared "adventure hour" and took their leave of us every night when we took our midnight lunch. Two of the youngest were musicians and they played together almost half the day, every day, while riding or resting. One had a concertina, the other a fiddle, and they played complex fast melodies the like of which I'd never heard.

The rest of the militia, to my surprise, accepted the youths' irresponsibility as inevitable. And while I overheard Nola complain occasionally, no one attempted to dampen their fun. Myself, I was quite happy for the levity they brought to the trip—they reminded me of my wild youth, the months I'd spent on the run from the Grinder.

No one knew quite what to do with me, that was plain. Some people treated me like a prisoner, others like a stranger. The oldest woman, Ekarna, was perhaps the cruelest of the bunch. It was plain she didn't trust me. But she wore a necklace of human teeth around her neck—a style I hadn't seen on anyone else—and I was reasonably sure the distrust was mutual.

On the third night we stopped at the ruins of Sotoris and I thought my heart was going to crawl out of my throat to lay among the ashen remains of the village. Many in our company wept as they picked through the rubble, and I longed for death in a more tangible way than I ever had, before or since. I had done this. I had destroyed an entire community. We didn't camp there, thank the heavens—I have no idea what I might have done.

Strangely, this sense of sin renewed my courage for the assault against the imperial forces—my newfound disregard as to whether I lived or died did wonders to steel my resolve. It was weeks or months more before the last sparks of my patriotism flickered out, but the burning of Sotoris and being sent to my death by Dolan

Wilder had certainly changed my priorities. As we rode across the mountains on frozen nights, I felt a hate growing in me I hadn't felt in years. I wanted to see Dolan Wilder die.

On the fourth day, as we camped under the leaves of an ancient maple grove, the youth with the concertina invited me to sit with him and his friends. They introduced themselves to me. There was Grem, who had invited me, and Dory, his sister. Joslek, a handsome and shy young man I felt just slightly too old for. Evana, the youngest, who played fiddle. And Desil. It was Desil whom I came to know the best the soonest. She was a heavyset woman with smart eyes and an aura of tight black curls that framed her head. She was without a doubt the wisest of them, and perhaps the wisest person I'd met, if you'll pardon me the risk of hyperbole. She couldn't have been more than seventeen.

"You cried last night in Sotoris," she said to me. "Why?"

I began to tell her about riding in with the man in the top hat, but she cut me off.

"I know about that—I was there, I saw you. All five of us grew up there. The Hollorots, the family they killed, were my second cousins. Yor, the kid with the open throat, was my friend. But you weren't the one who did it."

"I didn't stop them," I said.

"Neither did I," she replied.

Desil cut an apple in two with her boot knife and offered me half. I took it, bit into it. It was more tart than sweet, but ripe nonetheless and the juice ran down into my growing beard.

"You can have your guilt," she said, "if it makes you feel better. Or if you like the way that it makes you feel worse. Whatever it takes for you to learn to carve distance between yourself and the place you're from, from the soldiers who speak your mother tongue, that's alright. But when your guilt stops being useful, you'd better let it go. It can fester and ferment in your belly."

I nodded. Thereafter, I rode with her and her friends as often as with Sorros and Nola. I went with them on adventure hour, exploring frozen creeks and scrambling up rock walls in the light of the waning moon. I was older than them, but since I didn't seem to have a problem acting like a kid they didn't have a problem accepting me as one.

Grem was about my size, and he gave me some clothes—wool pants and a longshirt. They just call it a longshirt, it turns out. It felt good to get out of the uniform, but I held onto the greatcoat. The militia cloaks were just too formless for me.

One exceptionally cold night the six of us clambered up behind a frozen waterfall. My hands were so numb I barely felt it when a sharp rock cut through my glove and into my finger, but I'd have risked much worse for a chance of that view. I've never seen anything like it. The falls had become a single frozen sheet, a cascade of icicle lit by the waning moon, and behind it was a semicircle shelf carved out from the cliff by thousands of years of water.

Grem stalked around the cave with his concertina, listening to the acoustics, trying to find the best spot.

"Careful," Dory told him, as he walked up to the icy edge of the shelf, the frozen falls just out of reach beyond.

"Listen," he said, then played a few long, slow notes, the lowest on his instrument. They carried throughout the half-cave and I felt them in my bones. Then Grem picked up the tempo, started into a mournful song, then, over the course of minutes, transformed it into a happy reel. He was dancing.

Everyone was smiling but Dory, who watched her baby brother like a mother watches her child. When Grem slipped, she was up in an instant, lashing out her arm and catching him by the long-shirt. His hat went over the cliff.

Grem was suspended over the cliff's edge for a moment, and time was frozen like the waterfall. Then, with a deep breath that carried out into the night air, Dory dragged her brother back from the edge and onto the shelf.

The two collapsed.

"Shit," Grem said. "That was close."

"Be more careful," Dory said. "Please."

The moment between the two was so private that the rest of us—well, at least I—felt like intruders. I turned to Desil, beside me.

"I'll never figure out if I'm supposed to let worry get the best of me," she said. "Because I don't want to fall off a cliff but I don't want to risk never looking over the edge."

I wished I had some wisdom that had come from age to share with her, but I had none.

....

As we rode past landmarks, my young friends pointed them out to me. I learned a lot about the land from them, though I could never tell when they were speaking from experience or simply making things up. Either way, their sense of awe and excitement was infectious, and I think I came to love the mountains. Almost enough that, sometimes, I forgot we were marching to war. One day we built a sauna out of canvas tarps, steamed it with hot stones, then ran naked from the near-unbearable heat to jump naked into the near-unbearable cold of the Geris river. Another night, we stopped for midnight-lunch in an open field and watched a meteor shower.

I ran out of tobacco halfway through the trip, and only once the last pinch had gone into my lungs and out into the air did it occur to me that none of my companions smoked. I've never been one to smoke more than once or thrice a day, but running out made me all the more anxious.

The final night was grim. We all rode close together, and keeping calm became a full time endeavor for most of us. The moon was new. The stars were out, a tactical disadvantage, but looking at the constellations as we rode became my primary solace as the fear and anxiety turned my stomach into knots and my thoughts into nightmares.

We saw the cook fires from a half a mile out, at least a dozen of them burning in the camp—a clear contradiction to General Wilder's stated policy. We dismounted and tied our mounts to trees.

"Cut through her tether halfway," Nola told me as I secured the pony. "In case we can't return, she'll be able to tear herself free."

Two scouts returned and called us together, and the thirty of us formed a circle with two rows, the inner circle squatting, the outer circle standing. I stood in the outer row. Five people faced outwards, scanning the dark for enemies.

"We saw two sentries at the base of the path up the overlook," a man said, his dark skin darkened further by soot. "They've got a small fire and are playing cards. They might be drunk, too, but they're definitely awake."

"There's likely another pair watching the first," Ekarna suggested. I found myself nodding along with the rest of the Free Company.

"Doro will smell them out, and I'll cut their throats," a woman said. She patted a hound, presumably Doro.

"Flash a light when you're done, or if you can't find them," the first scout said, "and we'll take out the card players."

"The rest of us will wait just out of sight," Nola said. "If we hear gunfire or an alarm, we'll start the battle. Otherwise, we'll wait for you to get back and then creep closer."

Everyone nodded. In the starlight, faces were indistinguishable. What's more, many of the Company had begun to don their masks. Identity became unimportant.

"Objections?" someone asked. There were none.

"There are a hell of a lot more of them than there are of us," Nola said. Her voice took on a tone I'd never heard her use before—the General in her, I supposed. "Ten to one. But they're expecting us below, in the main camp, and we know they're up top, peering over the edge. So we'll be behind them, just give them a little push, and down they'll go. If at *any* point we find ourselves in a fair fight, I say we get out. Meet at yesterday's camp."

"Aye," someone said.

"Aye," more people murmured.

"We can do this," she said.

With that, the circle broke. Sorros handed me a balaclava and my old gun belt.

"If I lied?" I asked.

"You didn't lie," he responded. "But if you did, I'll kill you."

We moved forward as a group, crouched low to hide our silhouettes, until the scout motioned us to stop. A dog and three people disappeared into the trees, and we waited.

I want to describe to you what it felt like to wait there, knowing a signal meant both the start of the attack and that our advantage was lost. Knowing I was a combatant in what most people would consider not-my-war. But the words I have available don't seem adequate. Was I afraid? Perhaps. Was I excited? Most assuredly. Were my bowels loose and did bile rise in my throat? Of course.

My mind reached down towards that ember of hate in my belly—I wanted to stoke it up until it burned inside me. But I couldn't find it. And yet, I was part of something. When I couldn't find courage within myself I took it from the men and women around me. I had a pistol in hand and a mask over my face, and together we were going to kill a lot of people who probably needed to die.

No alarm went off, no gunshots rung out in the night. The same four silhouettes came back through the trees, and it was done—the guards had been silenced. We moved forward, up to the overlook.

Sorros, Nola, and I were at the back. On their own insistence, my young friends formed the vanguard.

I've no natural affinity for skulking through the underbrush, it turns out, and I spent so long disentangling myself from brambles that I was surprised I made it to the battle at all.

When we reached the clearing at the top of the overhang, we saw scores and scores of low tents, some pitched against the side of the earthen bunker, some in tight rings outside those. The mortars, to my relief, were manned but clearly facing down towards the camp below.

"Our job is simple but essential," Nola told Sorros and me. "We hang back, by this path, and shoot anyone in a uniform we see. We're keeping our own escape clear and preventing theirs."

I nodded. It didn't seem as simple as she made it sound, but I checked my pistol. I'd never fired one before in my life, but it seemed an inopportune time to bring up that detail. It was loaded, and I knew the basic idea.

Two shadowy torch-wielders bolted out from the trees from either end of the clearing and crossed over to the camp. Within seconds, the outermost tents were ablaze, and the four arsonists moved towards one another, lighting every scrap of canvas in their path. Before they met in the middle, twenty bandits and two dozen dogs tore out from the woods at a full run, screaming as they went. They broke into the camp and explosions went off.

Howls of anguish cut into the air. A burning man in his night-clothes came down the path towards us, but before I could lift my gun, Sorros had shot him dead.

I don't like gunfighting. I know that now. It has nothing in common with a street brawl. I don't like being shot at and, it turns out, I even more strongly dislike shooting at people. Particularly when you shoot those people in the face and then their face keeps the same expression as they fall over never to rise. Even when it's people I don't like very much. Even strangers. But I shot at maybe thirty people that night and I probably killed four or five of them.

I see the faces of the men I killed more clearly in my dreams then I ever did in life, but I don't wake full of fear or guilt, just perturbed.

The battle went on longer than I thought it would. Most of the enemy were slain or mortally wounded in the first attack, but some took refuge in the bunker.

It was near the end of it all that two more soldiers burst out of the smoldering tents towards the path we were covering. Nola shot one, but Sorros's rifle jammed as he drew bead on the second. I shot him from less than ten feet away and he crumpled to the ground. A third figure, a tall man, ran next. A muzzle flash lit his face—Wilder. I raised my gun and I'd like to think he even saw me, even recognized me. Sorros shot him in the heart and he fell backwards with a whimper that by rights I ought not have heard over the sounds of the battle.

I broke from the trees to run over to him. There he was, the man who had conquered Vorronia, dead on the mountain. He'd been laid low by a peasant with a captured rifle. He was in his night clothes, his top hat clutched under his arm.

I was through with hiding and strode into the field of combat. Inside the line of tents was a chaos unfit for the stories of hell. Men lay as broken corpses. A dog chewed at a man's face. Another dog stood over her dead master and howled. Two men shot at me. I killed one of them, I think, and the other one was shot down by a woman bleeding from her neck who could scarcely stand. I heard a blast and through the haze of smoke, I saw the militia forcing its way into a gap in the wall of the bunker. Desil led the charge and fell first, shot in the face by a man who was soon to die himself.

Within seconds it was over. The last remnants of His Majesty's forces came out with their hands above their heads and were stripped and guarded.

We had won. The dead were all around us, ours and theirs, and the wounded cried in pain or stared blankly at their wounds. So many of us had been injured—including me, it turned out. A bullet from one side or another had struck my right arm near the shoulder.

A cheer went up at the end of it all, a ragged thing, full-throated and loud and rasping. I joined in. Then I passed out.

Seven

The screaming woke me up, as did the cold, as did the pain. Daylight filtered in through the canvas walls of the medical tent and illuminated the scene next to me. Grem was thrashing on his cot not three feet away, held down by a pair of assistants including his sister Dory. Ekarna served as his surgeon, her earth-tone militia garb covered with a blood-soaked black apron. She had a bone saw in hand and was busy cutting off the young man's leg at the knee.

I lost it. I'd been fighting panic successfully for weeks, but it was too much for me. I fought for air with shallow breaths and was torn between flight and paralysis. Paralysis won. Under Grem's screams, I heard the grinding of saw against bone. I turned away and started shaking. The pain in my shoulder grew worse. Better to have pain than no arm. I tried to stand up but my mind wouldn't let me move.

A hand touched my shoulder—my good shoulder. "It's alright," Nola said to me.

"How is that" I managed, though I didn't turn to look at her. The screaming next to me stopped, replaced by a thick, panicked breathing.

"Ekarna has done this before," Nola told me. I'd been speaking, and especially reading, Vorronian since I was thirteen, but my language faculties had all but escaped me in the moment and it took me a long time to process her words. "She's a surgeon from Hronople, at the best hospital in Hron. And Grem's not in pain; the ether cuts it away."

"Screaming..." I said.

"Side effect of the ether," she said. It didn't help I'd never heard the word "side effect" in Vorronian before and had to figure it out from context. "Ether," fortunately, was a Vorronian word in the first place.

"I want my arm," I said.

"They aren't going to amputate your arm," Nola said. "You got lucky. The bullet went right through. And if you *stay* lucky and if you keep the wound clean, you'll keep your arm."

I turned over to face Nola. Behind her, Grem had passed out. The surgeon was done and was cleaning her tools at the wash basin. Dory held her brother's hand and stared at the place where Grem's leg had been.

I remembered Desil and I started to cry uncontrollably. Nola got uncomfortable and left me, but Dory took my hand in her free one and started to sob quietly as well.

Since I was conscious and not mortally wounded, I was asked to leave the hospital tent after Ekarna put a few black stitches across the entry and exit wounds and put my arm in a sling. Outside, I focused on my breathing, on the cloud of vapor that escaped my mouth with every breath. Around me, women and men saw to the tasks of hard-won victory.

At the final count, thirty of us, with twenty-four dogs, had killed one hundred and seven and captured twenty—which meant at least fifty had likely run off. Eight of our people were dead—Desil, Evana, Yormos, Talli, Astos, Reu, Molisha, and Lilt—as well as another six dogs. Twelve of us were wounded.

The prisoners were asked if they wished to bury their compatriots, but they refused. The dead soldiers, all but Wilder himself—were instead stacked with wood and burned in the largest and most vile fire I'd seen in my life. I'd call it a funeral pyre, but there wasn't a funeral. Sorros and another oversaw the release of the prisoners four at a time, in groups of two wounded and two fully-able, to make their way out of the Cerracs. Each was told that were they to return, they would never receive quarter again. Some looked thankful, others murderous, but they were released all the same.

One man, I believe the stablehand I'd met the first day of my arrival in the Cerracs, never took his eyes off of me. "We'll find you, Dimos Horacki," he said, his voice hoarse on account of the dog bite that had broken his collarbone, "and we'll kill you. Your family, back in Borolia? They'll hang even sooner."

For the first time in my life, I was glad the war had orphaned me.

"The Empire never forgives a traitor," he went on. "I'll watch you—"

The man never finished that sentence, however, because Nola put her pistol under his chin and fired, sending a fine spray of gore into the air. In perfect but charmingly accented Boroli, she announced, "If anyone else would like to threaten the lives of non-combatants, please do so now."

Unsurprisingly, no one did.

A captured Fourth Armsman pleaded his case to bring the body of Wilder with him when he left, but his request was denied unanimously. "We will salt his corpse," a woman told the officer in a thick accent. "Though the dead cannot suffer the same as the living."

It took most of the militia most of the day to dig far enough down in the rocky soil to bury our eight comrades, and as the sun went down we gathered to say our farewells.

"We are of the earth," Grem said, from a stretcher carried by two of his friends. "To the earth we will return." Dory threw her brother's leg into the grave. Ekarna unstrung a tooth from her necklace, kissed it, and threw it into the pit. Then together, everyone but the wounded buried the dead.

The corpse-fire was still smoldering on the overlook, so we moved our camp out to the forest.

I woke up sore and miserable. It was cold and I was lonely and I'd been dreaming of home. I dragged myself off the cot, into my wool overclothes, and into the morning air. Ekarna came by on her rounds and helped me back into my sling, admonishing me for having removed it to sleep.

"What needs doing?" someone asked at breakfast. Everyone was groggy and sleep deprived.

"We need to take inventory of stores, ours and theirs," someone suggested.

"We'll do it," Dory said, "Grem and I."

"Thank you," people said.

"I could use a few people to help me track down the soldiers who ran," a scout said. "Tail them for a bit, make sure they aren't regrouping for attack."

Several people volunteered.

The tasks were divvied up as people wolfed down sausage. Someone handed me a tin mug full of coffee—I hadn't had coffee since I'd been rescued by the militia. It was strong, black, and delicious.

Sorros and I volunteered to scavenge what we could from the

soldiers' main camp, and we helped load carriages with provisions and munitions and most of the assorted spoils of war. I took all the tobacco I found. But the journals of enlisted men were left untouched and most of what in the empire passes as "valuables" were left as well. I asked Sorros, and he explained.

"We'll take what we need from those we've killed, but no more. I can't imagine a reason I need a dead man's earrings any more than I need the letters he got from his wife. Maybe some friend of his will find these things and they'll one day find their way to his family, maybe not. I won't be the one to make certain they don't."

Wilder's belongings, however, were treated with no such reverence. We kept his logbooks and letters alike, and Sorros took to wearing his top hat. He was, as he pointed out, the man who brought down the scourge of the Cerracs. He offered me his old flat-top bowler, which I took gladly and have worn daily since. Later, I gave my old bowler to Grem.

"Are you a hero now, then?" I asked Sorros.

He grinned. "I'll be forgotten one day the same as you. I'm no hero. I just decided I get to the keep the hat."

But while Sorros was cheered from all corners, and my own standing in the Free Company of the Mountain Heather went up substantially, the real hero who had been made from my point of view that night was Desil Tranikfel, a sixteen-year-old warrior raised as a goatherd in the now-destroyed village of Sotoris. She had been a woman of uncommon bravery—and, however briefly, my friend.

When we came to my own tent, my trunk was gone. No matter, that. Finding a new suit was the least of my worries.

That night at dinner, the scouts returned with news that the deserters had not regrouped, but appeared to be making their way out of the mountains. Our talk turned to the future.

"So Dimos," someone asked me, "what's the King going to do now?"

I'd been thinking about that all day, and I had my answer ready. "His Majesty will declare Wilder a hero and the city will mourn. The newspapers will drum up popular opinion against you all—against us—and sometime, maybe this spring, maybe this summer, they'll march in with cannons to 'civilize' this place. It won't be pretty."

"How many will come?" someone asked.

"His Majesty commands a peacetime ground force of thirty thousand, down from one hundred thousand at the peak of the Vorronian war, most of whom could be called back to active duty. If he mobilizes his navy, that's another twenty thousand."

This news was not well-received. Around the fire, faces looked grim.

"There are only one hundred thousand people in all of Hronople," Sorros said, "and only that same number again in all the villages, towns, and smallholdings together."

"How many troops can you mobilize?" I asked.

"We're not 'troops,'" Ekarna replied. "We're free women and men."

"How many will fight?" I asked.

"There're around two thousand of us armed and trained in the militias," Sorros answered. "And most able-bodied adults will fight if pressed."

"A peasant with a spear is no match for calvary," someone argued.

"We'll have to get them guns," someone replied.

"So they can accidentally shoot themselves?" someone suggested.

"There're five, ten thousand people in Karak," Dory said. "And I doubt they want the empire here any more than Hron does."

"Fuck Karak," Sorros said.

"Karak?" I asked, but no one answered me.

And so it went. In the face of the overwhelming odds against them, the Free Company of the Mountain Heather, so recently victorious, fell into bickering.

"There's nothing for it," Nola said. "We have a few months to raise an army and drive them off. There might be fifteen or a hundred thousand soldiers marching against us, but that doesn't change what we need to do."

"The General's right," Dory said. "We can rally Hron to war."

"We can attack them first, set fire to their crops and houses," someone else recommended.

"We can fortify the mountain passes," Grem suggested.

"We could surrender," Sorros said.

Nola looked at him as though he were a stranger. "You want to give up?" she asked.

"No," Sorros replied. "I don't think we should. I think we should fight them until they break our bones with artillery and even then I think we should make the splintered bits of our body pierce their flesh and paint the snow red with their arterial blood. But I don't want us to rule out any possibilities yet. For two reasons: one, if we think of it, then someone else we're trying to convince to fight will think of it too. If we think it's a terrible idea we need to be prepared to tell them why. And two, well, it's *probably* not what we want to do, but *it might be*. And just because it's 'weak,' doesn't mean it might not at some point be the smartest plan."

"I like the part where even our bones try to kill them," Nola said. "I think that's a better plan."

"Those of the Free Company of the Mountain Heather will fight the agents of the Empire until, if not beyond, their dying breath?" someone suggested.

"Is that a proposal?"

"It is."

"Objections?" someone asked.

None were raised.

"We're agreed?" Dory asked.

"Agreed," people said.

"Then let's figure out some really good ways to murder imperialists," Nola said, and everyone laughed.

There's no distinction in Cer, in turns out, between "to murder" and "to kill." There's only one verb for both concepts. To this day, I'm not sure if that is a political statement or an oversight. Nor am I convinced I know which meaning Nola meant that night as the flames of the campfire licked the mountain air.

The rest of the night was spent brainstorming, clearly a favorite pastime among the Free Company. Eventually, the seriousness of the proposals faded, and, sometime after Dory suggested dressing up ostriches in Imperial uniforms to spread rumors that we were witches who could polymorph men into animals, I went off to my tent to set down my notes by lamplight. They wanted a journalist, and I had plenty to write.

An hour later, I cut the light and lay on my back, my hands under my head. It took me a long time to fall asleep. A month prior, I'd woken up every morning in the twilight to walk to work a job I'd hated for a man I could scarcely abide. A fortnight prior, I'd been in the company of the worst men I'd ever met. But just then? Just then I felt free. Tired and scared and wounded and free.

Eight

I woke with a start to the report of nearby gunfire. Six, maybe seven shots in rapid succession, both rifle and pistol fire. My tent was dark, so I threw open the flaps and saw a muzzle flash from the tree line as a rifle went off. I reached for my pants, changed my mind, and simply pulled on my boots—to walk barefoot on a January night in the mountains was likely as dangerous as the gunfight. I left the tent in just a union suit, my loaded revolver held slack at my side.

And immediately, a hand covered my mouth. A pistol pressed into my temple. My unseen attacker jerked me backwards, pulling me off my feet, and started toward the tree line. My wound re-opened, and I cried out instinctively.

"Shout again, rat," my captor said, in refined, upperclass Boroli. "I'd love the excuse to put you down."

I heard a galloping horse and the thick sound of a sword cutting flesh, and the pistol dropped from my head. My captor collapsed behind me, his hand on my face pulling me down on top of him. I pried myself free and rolled away, shivering.

By firelight, I saw Ekarna on a horse, bloody saber in her hand.

I turned to the tree line and saw three men in the green-and-gold. I emptied my revolver into one while he fired into the camp, and soon the other two fell as well. Two militia—in the dark I couldn't tell who—ran up to the woods.

"Clear!" Nola cried out.

"Report!" Ekarna called, dismounting. The Free Company gravitated naturally to the only campfire still burning, the watch fire. Three scouts with dogs went off into the woods, and five people faced outwards while the rest faced inwards.

"We're all here," Sorros said. "So there's that at least."

"They came for me," I said. "I'm a traitor."

"Is that how you see yourself?" Nola asked.

"I don't know," I said. "Maybe. But I don't know that I owe an empire allegiance simply by accident of birth." It was the first time I'd thought of it that way.

Nola nodded at that.

"It was four men we released," a scout reported on returning. "They must have circled around after we checked on them."

"We can't stay here," Dory said. "We're in no shape for a fight."

"Anyone hurt?" Ekarna asked.

"My wound re-opened," I said, and no one else spoke up.

So Ekarna and I left the circle for the hospital tent. The old surgeon lit a lantern and began to clean and re-stitch my wound.

"Thank you," I said.

"You're welcome," she replied.

I was silent for awhile, fighting off the worst of the pain.

"I know you don't like me much," I began.

"You're fine. I just don't trust you, is all. It's hard to trust a turncoat."

"Is there anything I can do?" I asked.

She sighed. "No, honestly, there's not. You're probably a per- fectly fine young man and I'm glad you did what you did. You saved my life by warning us about the ambush as sure as I saved yours tonight. It's just a thing, I don't know. It's probably not fair to you, either."

"It's not like the other side ever saw me as one of them either."

"That's true, I'm sure. And for the young folks here, they get it—they get what you said, about not owing allegiance to the side of a fight on which you're born. But for me? For me I guess I think you *do*. I guess I'm just old-fashioned. Though if you're a turncoat, at least you're *our* turncoat. And any chance I'll get, I'll try to keep you alive. Just make sure your coat-turning days are over."

She cut the thread and started on the exit wound on the back of my shoulder.

"Whose teeth are those?" I asked, nodding towards her necklace.

She laughed, the first time I saw her do that. "Would you believe me if I told you that they're the teeth of men I've killed?" she asked.

"Yes," I answered.

She laughed again, this time hard enough she had to stop sew- ing me up for a second.

"They're my dead wife's teeth," she said. "Sorros's birth mother. Maybe it seems macabre to you, but it's what we used to do, where I'm from."

"You're Sorros's—" I began.

"I'm his birth mother's wife, yes. Which makes me his mother too. And if you say we're anything alike I'll stick my fingernail into your bullet hole."

I grinned. She finished patching me up, then made me tea. "For the wound," she said, "and for your nerves." While I sipped on the mug of strong, bitter medicine, she walked me to my tent. At the tent flap, she handed me a leather pouch of herbs, told me to chew on them then apply them as a poultice at least once a day when I changed the dressing. She also handed me a pouch of opium, for the pain.

"A bullet wound is a puncture and a burn both," she said. "And it goes deep. If you get a bacterial infection in there, you'll be lucky if you only lose your arm. So keep it covered and clean if you want to live."

Then she clasped my hand goodnight, called me a turncoat, and went off to her tent.

....

I slept well that night, thanks to the opium. My wound only hurt violently if I did something as stupid as move it, lie on it, or think about it.

In the morning, we were off. The closest to consensus we'd reached the night before was that we couldn't stay where we were. Some of the Company wanted to return to their base camp and continue to patrol the area. Others wanted to rebuild Sotoris. For my own part, Nola and Sorros talked me into accompanying them on a recruitment drive of sorts. We were on our way to Hronople to call for a council of war.

It took no urging to make me see the advantages of this plan. I longed to see more of Hron, and more so I longed for a warm bath and the chance to shave. A cold front was moving in and I had no plans to get stuck in the militia camp for months on end.

I mounted a blue roan we'd taken from the enemy. I'd grown quite accustomed to life in the saddle, I was proud to say, and I chose the roan because it reminded me of the one I'd ridden that first morning on my way to the Imperial camp. What I hadn't anticipated, however, was how every step of the way would send knives of pain into my wound. With Nola's help, I tied myself into the saddle in case I were to pass out.

Dory and Grem came with us. Grem, as much as he hated to admit it, was out of the war, and Dory had only joined the Company to see her younger brother stay safe. The whole recruitment drive idea was Nola's, but as a foreigner herself she wouldn't get far without Sorros. And Sorros, for his part, seemed happy enough to get out of the snow.

We said our goodbyes to the rest of the Company. Grem and Dory tried to convince Joslek to join us, but failed. He wanted to fight, he said. Half his friends had died at the hands of the invaders, and anything that delayed his chance to open fire on the gold-and-green was simply unacceptable.

Ekarna gave Grem and me more healing herbs, clean bandages, and strict instructions to keep our wounds clean and away from stress. She told Grem to find his way to Hronople within a month or two so he could be fitted with a prothesis.

We brought five horses for the five of us, though Grem and Dory rode double. The extra mount carried provisions. Two of the dogs came with us. Sampson, a huge black beast, and Sampson's mottled sister Damsel—named ironically in Boroli. I took to calling them Sammit and Dammit, because that's what Dory called them. The two animals were a great comfort to have at our sides.

"Winter comes late in the Cerracs," Sorros told me as we rode.

"This isn't winter?" I asked.

"It's only January," Sorros replied. "The real snow will hit soon, and we'll stable the horses until snowmelt. People who have to will get around on skis and everyone else will stay indoors. Most riders caught in blizzards never return, and too many of those who do have eaten their horses. Avalanches, come early spring, are worse. My grandmother claims an entire village once got swallowed in snow, and it's not uncommon to lose a homestead somewhere in Hron every year. In the city, though, it's not so bad... the geothermal vents warm most of the houses and the covered walkways."

I nodded, though I didn't really understand. I was Borolian... what did I know of winter?

"You trying to scare the foreigners?" Dory asked.

"No," Sorros said.

"If you change your mind, let me know."

We made it to the main road soon enough, which was beginning to feel familiar to me. There, to the right, was the snag of a behemoth aspen tree. To the left, a trio of granite boulders loomed over the road and cast long shadows in the evening. We passed over three bridges in rapid succession, each built of stone and seemingly as old as the earth on which we rode.

"So where are we headed?" I asked.

"Moliknari," Nola said. "It's a village maybe three days uphill from here."

Sorros shook his head. "We should start in Holl. Moliknari is too small—it's not worth our time."

"Moliknari is closer, and they're hosting the midwinter festival next week."

"No one from Moliknari will fight," Sorros said. He was agitated. I'd never seen him agitated. "They're just hill trash. Can't tell a gun from a spear."

"Hill trash? Aren't *you* hill trash?" Nola asked, her voice beginning to raise slightly.

"I am," Sorros said, his voice going soft. "And I'm from Moli-knari. And I don't think we—especially I—should go there any-time soon. It might not be safe."

We rode on for a minute or so in silence, the hoofsteps keeping time.

"Alright, we'll go to Holl," Nola conceded.

"Don't we have a say in this?" Dory asked.

"Of course," Nola said. "What do you think?"

"I actually don't really care," Dory said. "I just wanted to make sure we got a say in it."

"Well, I think—" Grem started.

"No one cares what *you* think, Grem," Dory said.

Grem laughed, and I think I saw him smile for the first time since the battle.

"I think we should camp somewhere pretty tonight," Grem said. "Even if we could press on further. I think we should camp by a waterfall, or in a grove of ancients."

....

Sorros Ralm found us both. In the mid-afternoon we left the main road for a game trail that took us past the edge of the forest and into the older trees. As Sorros explained, most mature forests are only dense and tangled in the outer ten or fifteen feet. Further in, less sunlight hits the ground, so less can grow and things open up significantly. We rode through ferns and over moss-blanketed logs until we reached an open glade towered over by twenty ancient oaks. Not far off, we heard the dull roar of a small waterfall.

As soon as we came to a stop, I slid from my horse exhausted. My shoulder was killing me and I felt weaker than ever. Dory helped her brother down from their horse and he and I laid in the grass, thankful for the cessation of motion. We smoked opium and let the others string the tarps, begin dinner, and raise the food stores above bear-height from a tree branch.

Dammit came and curled up between the two of us, perfectly positioned so I could scratch her head while Grem scratched right above her tail.

"Why am I happy?" Grem asked me.

"What do you mean?" I asked.

"Ekarna cut my leg off yesterday. No, not yesterday. The day before? I don't know. It doesn't matter. Ekarna cut my leg off and I watched her do it. And Evana, and Desil… I shouldn't be happy."

"Grief comes in waves," I said. Six years older than my friend, I was trying to be wise. I thought about losing my parents in the war. "It comes in waves because you should get to be happy sometimes."

"We killed those bastards," Grem said. I don't know if he'd heard me or not. "Didn't we? We shot every fucking one of those motherfuckers who came into Hron like they could do anything they want."

"We did," I said.

"That makes me happy," Grem said. "And the waterfall, I can hear the waterfall. I don't think I even need to see it. I can hear it. And those trees. And tonight we'll get stars."

"I've read that in the Floating Isles," I said, "people believe that when you die, your spirit picks a star, or is picked by a star or something, and you join it. It burns your soul, and the brightest stars are the ones that are burning the most people. I think it's supposed to be a good thing."

Grem laughed. "In Hron, I guess we each believe something different."

"What do you believe?" I asked.

"I think my friends are just dead," he said. "The only thing left of them is this conversation, their corpses rotting in the ground, and the bits of freedom we gained through their deaths."

"Bits of freedom sounds like a good legacy to me," I said.

"I'd prefer a heaven," Grem said. "I don't want to die."

"Then don't for awhile," I told him.

Grem laughed.

....

But the stars didn't come out that night. The clouds, instead, rolled in. We ate our dinner—oats with honey and fried yams and beets—around the fire, mostly feeling cold and tired.

"It's going to storm," Nola said.

"No it's not," Sorros replied.

"Yes it is," Nola said.

"No it's not," Sorros said.

"Shut up," Dory said. "Both of you. I'm tired and my everything hurts so you two need to shut up about it."

They shut up about it. We talked a bit longer, but with little joy, and soon curled up in our bags to sleep in a circle around the fire.

The storm hit before dawn. The wind woke the dogs, and the dogs woke us. The first flakes of snow fell heavy and wet and by the time the sun was rising, there was a foot of snow on the ground.

"What do we do?" I asked, while Nola rekindled the fire.

"Gather wood," Sorros answered. "As much as we can before it's buried. Hang more canvas, turn our pavilion into a tent. Get our horses in, it's going to be cramped."

"If you have gods," Nola said, "I'd suggest prayer."

"I wouldn't take you for a woman who believes in the power of prayer," I said.

"I believe in the power of prayer to keep panic at bay in those who believe in the gods," Nola said.

"We've got enough food for another four or five days," Sorros said, "but a lot less if the horses can't graze and we've got to feed them."

"We're not killing the horses," Dory said.

"Not yet," Nola agreed.

"Enough of this shit," Grem said. The rest of us had stood, but he, for his injury, was still in his bag. "Get to work!"

I volunteered to help Dory re-hang the tarps while Nola and Sorros went off looking for wood. I fumbled with knots through my thick wool glove, resorting to my teeth since I had only one good hand. The wind was vicious, and soon I was shivering.

"We'll be fine," Dory said to me, putting a hand on my back.

My mother used to do that. She used to put a hand on my back when she was reassuring me. Even when it was about something she didn't believe herself.

It took us hours to get walls on the pavilion and the horses inside. I was soaked. On Grem's advice, I built up the fire, stripped off my clothes to dry, and curled up under blankets. In minutes, I was asleep, though I woke up several times in the night, convinced every sound in the forest was someone who wanted me dead.

....

The storm raged the entire day, and by evening visibility outside the tent had dropped to nothing. The horses were agitated and so were we. Only Sammit and Dammit, bred for just such conditions, kept up their spirits.

Long after I'd shut down from pain and cold and fear, though, Nola, Sorros, and Dory kept up their work. They packed the snow outside into windbreaks, taking shifts to warm themselves by the fire. Nola saw to the horses. Sorros cooked three meals. And while the winds howled outside, while trees cracked under the weight of snow and crashed to the ground around us, Dory read books to her brother.

By dinnertime, we had a cozy home, and for a moment during dinner I managed to forget my predicament and tried to turn back into a journalist.

"Can I ask you about Hron?" I asked everyone after I'd cleaned my plate of winter greens and oats.

"Sure," Dory said.

"Well, then, what is it?"

Nola smiled. Dory laughed.

"You've fought for it," Dory said, "But I guess you don't know the first thing about it?"

"I think it's a country I accidentally invaded," I replied. This got a laugh from everyone.

"Hron's a country, I guess," Sorros said, "in that we're a collection of people with a somewhat-shared culture who commonly defend certain rough borders and principles. But we're not a country like Vorronia or Borolia or even the Floating Isles. We don't have a king or a parliament or a council or a royal priesthood or trade barons or capitalists or really any of the vestiges of power at all. We're a country, but we're an anarchist country."

"What does that mean?" I asked.

"It means that everyone in Hron is the master of their own destiny," Sorros said. "It means that there are no laws here, no prisons."

Dory chimed in. "The Free Confederation of Hron is a voluntary association of autonomous groups and individuals who cooperate to provide one another mutual aid," Dory said.

"Yeah, that mouthful right there. That's Hron. We're people who have each other's backs because having someone's back means someone has yours, and that's a good way to live."

"Why doesn't anyone know you exist?" I asked. "We talk about the Cerracs like it's just, I don't know, unaffiliated villages."

"What's so wrong with unaffiliated villages that makes them just crying out to be taken over or burned to the ground?" Grem asked.

"Hron's only a few years older than me," Sorros said. "And while *any* country is more of an idea than a physical thing, I think that's especially true here. People have been living in the Cerracs for centuries at least. Moliknari, where I'm from, we've got records going back a thousand years. But we didn't have a *country* until the Western War started. The failed revolutionists from Vorronia poured into the Cerracs and founded Hronople. They called for a great council, and people from every town and village in the mountains arrived. The council met for two years and hammered out the Hron Accord."

"Is that your constitution?" I asked.

"I... I guess," Sorros said. "I don't think that's the best word for it. I like 'accord.' But the Hron Accord sets out the principles of unity that bind us together. Anyone—any individual person, any group of people—can be part of Hron if they abide by the guidelines set out in the accord."

"And those who don't?"

"Most people do," Sorros said. "But those who don't want to associate with others by those principles are more than free to associate with others in whatever way they want, just not here, and not with us."

"So follow the rules or you're banished?" I asked.

"The rules don't say 'give us your three best ostriches every season,'" Sorros said. "They don't even say 'don't ever kill anyone,' not really. They're not the same as your laws. You're looking at this from the viewpoint of a Borolian."

"Well, what *do* they say?" I asked. I was growing defensive, and for some reason became committed to outing the hypocrisy of the anarchist.

"I actually don't remember," he said.

"I don't really either," Dory said. Nola and Grem were just smiling.

"You don't remember the rules? You don't remember the accord that you hold people to?"

"No," Sorros said, "I don't. The rules don't really matter. It's the spirit that matters, I think."

"Where I'm from, in Sotoris," Dory said, "we kind of remembered it like this: don't do anything horrible, and if you do something horrible, own up to it."

"I do remember that someone tried to amend the accord, about a decade ago," Sorros said. "They wanted to add a provision to the bottom, explicitly forbidding anyone from getting too hung up on the specifics of the accord."

"Did it pass?" I asked.

"You know," Sorros said, "I don't remember!"

Everyone was laughing at that, but I wasn't convinced. The Free Company of the Mountain Heather had operated efficiently enough without a central command, but there had been thirty of them. I couldn't imagine a country doing the same. They had laws, I was sure of it. They were likely just embarrassed about them.

....

The storm broke that night, and the sudden silence roused me. I'd been sleeping lightly, regardless—the day cooped up in the tent had left me restless—and I put on my greatcoat and stepped out of the tent. The snow was up to my mid-thigh.

Dory was there, leaning on his crutches, staring at the sky with his opium pipe in his mouth. I joined him, and looked up into the heavens.

"Do you think my leg is up there too, burning in one of the stars?" he asked. "It's buried in the same hole as my friends, after all."

I didn't answer him, but instead stared at the majesty above us.

"I think I'm going to call that one my leg-star," he said, pointing. "That one there, in the Sower's leg. It's kind of dim. I hope when I die I go to it instead of some other star."

"You don't actually believe any of this, do you?" I asked.

"No," he said.

"That's good," I said.

"But it's kind of pretty to think about," he said.

"I think you just summed up religion," I told him.

He smiled politely, then crutched back to the tent, leaving me with the heavens.

I looked up at Huros, the sailor, my favorite constellation, high up in the sky in midwinter. I looked at his two eyes, the twin stars, equally bright, one white, one gold. I thought about my parents, and I started to cry. I thought about everything I'd seen, and I cried harder. I wailed in the snow, among ancient oaks in the Cerracs, crying for the souls of the dead.

I'm a terrible atheist.

Nine

In the morning, over grits, we talked over our options.

"If we're going to ride," Nola said, "we've got to leave soon. When the snow forms a crust, it's bad news for the horses. They can cut their legs breaking through the ice. And we can't ride hard or they'll sweat too much and freeze."

"I think we need to go to Moliknari," Sorros said.

"I agree," Nola said.

"What happens if we try for Holl instead?" I asked.

"We run out of food, kill our horses, and probably freeze to death in the snow or at the very least they leave us wounded behind," Grem said. "Is that a fair estimation?"

"Yeah," Dory said, "pretty much."

"So what's the problem with Moliknari?" I asked.

"I'm from there," Sorros said.

"So?"

"You're from Borol, right? Imagine how welcome you are there at the moment."

"I hardly expect you sold your country out to some anarchists in the hills," I said. I started laughing, because I'm an idiot. "What did you do? Break the 'accord?'"

"That's enough," Nola said. She moved to sit beside her partner and put her hand on his knee. "He clearly doesn't want to talk about it. Whatever they think of him in Moliknari, we'll deal with it."

"I'm sorry," I mumbled, then filled my mouth with dried berries and turned away.

"I've always wanted to see Moliknari," Grem said. "And I haven't been to a midwinter festival in, I don't know, three years?"

"What's in Moliknari?" I asked.

"A lot of people there still follow the old ways," Grem said.

"A lot of people there are raving lunatics you mean," Sorros interjected.

"Old ways... like Ekarna and her necklace of teeth?" I asked.

"Oh, that's the least of it," Grem said. "They've still got worship in Moliknari, from what I hear. With sigils and effigies and everything."

"And madwomen and madmen who set themselves alight on the midsummer, too, is that it Grem?" Sorros asked.

"Well I heard—" he started.

"I don't doubt you've heard a lot of things about where I'm from. Worship or no, it's just a place—filled with people, some crazy some sane."

"Where I'm from," I said, "anyone who said you could get by without a formal government would be called crazy, deluded, or idealistic."

Grem grinned. "Maybe we're all three!"

....

There's no reason I can really explain as to why riding in deep snow is as tiring as it is. It might be the slow pace, it might be worrying about icy patches that could drop the horse. It might be just how damn cold it is.

Grem pulled out his concertina when we stopped for lunch, the first time I'd seen it in his hands since the battle. He began to play a song, a fast and happy song, but stopped before he finished the first bar. He tried a slower song, a mournful song, but made it no further. He threw the instrument into a snowdrift, then tried to stand up. Even with his crutch, he failed, and fell into the snow. Dory was with him in a second, helping him to his feet, and I heard his sobbing cries.

I went and retrieved the concertina, brushing it dry with my wool coat.

"Leave it," I heard Grem cry out.

He collapsed into Dory's arms and wept. Dory brushed his hair with her hand and looked out across the snowscape, her face unreadable. It was a long time before we were back on the march. I packed the concertina with my things.

....

On the morning of the fourth day since the storm, we drank a thin soup of snowmelt, wild winter greens, and rabbit bones for breakfast. We mounted our weary horses and began the day's journey. Grem and I had run out of opium, and I passed out from the pain at least once while we rode.

Two hours later, we saw Moliknari. It was larger than any town I'd seen in the mountains, with hundreds of buildings. The houses, however, were like those I'd seen anywhere else in Hron, built of stone and timber with steeply-pitched roofs.

"Wait here," Sorros said, then started to ride towards town.

"No," Nola said. "We won't let you go alone."

"Our entire reason for being here depends on you earning their respect. If you ride in with me, that might not be possible."

"Don't care," Nola said. "I won't pretend I don't know you."

Sorros looked at the rest of us, and one at a time we nodded.

"You're idiots," he said. "Solaritious to a fault." We don't have an adjectival form of the word "solidarity" in Boroli, but they have it in Cer and they use it all the time. "At least keep your guns hidden so they don't think you're like, thugs from Karak I've hired to keep me safe."

I looked to Nola, and since she was unbuckling her gun belt I did the same. She took her pistol and put it in her saddlebag, which she left unbuckled. We rode into town.

When I'd ridden into towns with the army, most all the villagers had waited for us in the central square, terrified. That February morning, when I rode into town with just the five us, there was a welcoming committee of twenty gathered on the central square, armed and calm.

"Hey everyone," Sorros said, dismounting ten yards away and walking forward with his hands held out to the side.

"Sorros Ralm," an elderly woman said from where she stood at the front of the crowd, no trace of affection in her voice.

"Marly Ghostmother," Sorros replied.

"What did I say to you, last time we spoke?" Marly held a short-barreled rifle slack at her side.

"That if you saw me again you might shoot me," Sorros said.

"And here you are," she said. "You think you're a hero now that you're a militiaman?"

"I do not," Sorros replied.

"Then why, by the Mountain, am I looking at you?"

"We were waylaid by the storm," Sorros said. "I had no intention to ride home."

"This isn't your home, Ghostmaker."

Sorros bowed his head.

"If you're here, Sorros, then you're to stay three days in my house, from now until the start of midwinter. Your friends are welcome in the guest hall. Is this amenable?"

"It is," Sorros said, raising his head, color returning to his face.

Marly turned from us and walked away, and Sorros followed. He took his top hat from his head and held it at his side. That was the last I saw of him until the festival.

"Anarchists are kind of strange," I said to Nola, in Boroli.

"You're onto something there," she replied.

....

I'd assumed they were great halls—in every town we'd gone through, there'd been a single large hall somewhere near the center of everything. I'd assumed they were for weddings and feasts, for the ruler or rulers to make decisions or live. I'd assumed wrong—they were guest halls. Our host Sakana, a young woman in practical clothing with a streak of white in her light brown hair, explained everything to us.

Moliknari's guest hall was the most impressive I'd seen thus far, a three story mansion built with ancient timbers and stones as tall as people. We walked in through the ornately inlaid doors and into a clean and hospitable open dining hall, with hearths in three of the stone walls and a circular stair leading up to balcony floor above us. We stood in the colored light of a stained glass abstract that cast strange colors over our faces and bodies.

"The guest hall doesn't belong to the town," Sakana explained at my questioning. "Artisans from nearby villages build them over the course of a summer or two, and they're meant to represent the pinnacle of their craft. In its way, the guest hall is the symbol of our allegiance to all of Hron: residents of Moliknari won't step foot into them. They're for visitors only. Well, except for the caretakers. We can go in, of course."

"What got you the job of caretaker?" I asked.

"I chose it, the same as anyone chooses a job."

"What if you didn't want to do it?" I asked.

"Then I wouldn't do it."

"And someone else would take your place?" I asked.

"If they wanted," she replied.

"What if no one wanted to caretake the guest hall?" I asked.

Sakana looked at my travel companions for reassurance that they knew I was clearly a madman.

It was Dory who answered my question. "If Sakana stepped down and no one stepped up, the guest hall would go unmaintained. People would bring it up that every now and then at council, and if someone decided it seemed like a useful or pleasurable thing to do, they'd take over."

"What if no one wanted to, I don't know, harvest food or tend to the ostriches or cook or wash up?" I asked.

Sakana was exasperated by my questioning.

"I'm sorry," I said to her, though I intended for my apology to extend to my companions as well. "I'm here as a journalist and the place I'm from is very, very different from Hron. I don't understand the way you live."

"If people wanted to starve, I suppose they could," Sakana said. "I tend to find that people prefer to eat. And to eat, we have to plant and harvest, we have to herd and hunt. We find joy in doing things for ourselves and our communities."

"What about less pleasant things, like washing dishes? Or, I don't know, maintaining your systems of sewage? Cleaning latrines?"

"Where you're from, do you have to get paid to shower? Dress yourself? When you're done working, do you walk off and leave the tools in disarray? I don't mean to sound disrespectful," Sakana said, "but are you a country of children?"

"No," I said.

"Well, since you're a grown man, while you're a guest at Moliknari, I'll expect you to clean up your own waste and wipe your own ass."

"I meant no offense," I said.

"Then make none," she answered.

Sakana led us to the back of the hall, through a door to a hallway with at least a dozen rooms leading off of it. "These are the quarters. You've got the run of the place for the moment, but you'll have to share when more people arrive for midwinter." Sakana turned to look at me. "You do know how to share, where you're from?"

I grew angry, but chose not to express it. "Yes," I said.

"The water closet is the last door on the right. If you make a mess of it, clean it up. I'll start cooking dinner at sundown this evening, and could use a hand or two to help in the kitchen."

With that, Sakana turned and walked down the steps.

"That didn't go well," I observed.

"Moliknari," Dory suggested.

"Not everyone likes foreigners," Nola said.

"Aren't you a foreigner?" I asked her.

"Used to be," she answered. "Ten years on, I'm just a girl with an accent. And listen—not everyone likes foreigners and more than that, not everyone likes journalists. Not everyone likes knowing that anything they say might end up in some book some day—or worse, as propaganda for the enemy."

"That's fair," I said. "I'll try to be more careful."

Nola put her hand on my shoulder. "For what it's worth, I don't think you pissed her off, just frustrated her. It's like someone coming into Borolia and asking you why you work for a living. It just doesn't make any sense to her. Hronople is a city of immigrants, but Moliknari has been living this way for hundreds of years."

"Alright," I said, and we went into our rooms.

....

Within hours of arriving in town, I discovered the wonders of Hronish bathing technology. In Borol, I thought I'd been doing well—the coal-fired furnace in my apartment at home had doubled as a water heater, and I'd been able to take a shower almost anytime I wanted. In Moliknari, however, the hot water pipes themselves warmed the building, and the slate floor of the generous bathroom was comfortably warm on my feet. The water was kept hot through any number of methods, including absorbing the heat of the sun while in greenhouse walls and, perhaps most ingeniously of all, by utilizing the excess heat put off by composting waste. Charcoal and wood served as backup fuel sources for heating the water and buildings, but this was rarely used outside the dead of winter. And to top it off, the water from the shower drain was used for greenhouse irrigation.

I hadn't taken a real shower since leaving Borol, and it was natural that, with hot water flowing over me, my thoughts turned back to the home I'd left, the home I was certain I would never be welcomed to again. I tried to get nostalgic and sad, I really did. A sort of pitiful thing to try to do, but I felt like a monster for not missing the place, so I tried to and failed. There were things here and there I could summon up memories of with longing: the fog rolling in from the harbor, the music in the streets, a few of the men I'd known; but no sooner had I settled my mind on one of these things than I remembered being a kid watching the rich feed their scraps to the dogs while my stomach had churned with hunger. I remembered sitting in the endless pool of hacks at the *Review*, writing about things I couldn't care less about just so I might be given the dignity of not starving. And I remembered the police, the armed men who roamed the streets enforcing laws they couldn't even recite, who killed with impunity.

Still, I miss the fog. And the people. Borol is a beautiful place—it's a shame about the way it's run.

I got to shave, with a mirror and warm water and everything. It was nice to see my chin again. And it felt good to sleep behind real walls that kept the winter winds at bay. It felt good to have some privacy. At long last, in the guest hall of Moliknari, I felt like I'd left the front.

Alone and warm for the first time in weeks, I started to think through my situation. I'd been cast along by the winds so long I had a hard time figuring out what I actually wanted to do. I wanted to see more of Hron, I knew that. I wanted to see Hronople. And I probably couldn't go home. The country was founded by refugees—maybe they had room for one more.

I laid off the questioning, and soon Sakana warmed up to me and my companions, hitting it off particularly well with Dory. The two disappeared for hours at a time every afternoon. Grem was quite content to spend most of his time reading in his room to give his leg a rest, so Nola and I wandered the village ourselves.

We spent most of our time at a small, unnamed cafe, sitting in a window nook and watching the snow fall lightly in the wind. I drank a lot of *carsa*, a black tea infused somehow or another to be as strong as coffee, and I ate a lot of biscuits and other baked goods sweetened with honey. The local scones—or the closest they had to scones—were flavored with foreign and bitter herbs, but they went well with the carsa. After so long at war, it was bliss.

The old man who ran the cafe, who went only by his surname Blosik, took to joining us at the table. He was jovial to a fault and every time he drank, his white drooping mustache sopped up as much carsa as he got into mouth. Townsfolk came in and out throughout the day to drink tea, catch up on news, or eat a light meal, and it was altogether a frightfully pleasant place.

True to Sakana's prophecy, we washed our own dishes before taking our leave each evening, and though Blosik protested that we need not do so, he showed us to the dish pit readily enough.

"Why do people call you General?" I asked Nola one day.

"It's a misnomer, really," Nola said. "I never made it past Second Lieutenant."

"You were in the war, then?" I asked.

Nola nodded.

"What brought you to Hron? Sorros?"

"Wish it had been Sorros. No, it was another man. He called himself Hideon, which probably wasn't his real name. I asked what his last name was one time, and he looked thoughtful, then told me his full name was 'Hideon Hideon.' He was a Vorronian revolutionary, an anarchist, born in Tar but trained in sabotage at a camp in the countryside."

"Doesn't Hideon mean—" I started.

"'Devil,' I guess you could say, that's probably the best translation," Nola finished for me. "But a sort of childlike devil. An imp.

Regardless, he was a saboteur, working for the dream of the revolution that had failed five years before he'd been born. I caught him on the side of the palace ship, ten pounds of black powder in a sack in his hand. That's how I made Second Lieutenant, actually."

"And?" I asked. "You fell in love with him?"

"I did," Nola said, laughing. "Though to be honest I was probably more in love with his ideals. I sprung him and another ten of his comrades and used my rank to smuggle them into Hron."

"Where is he now?" I asked.

"Oh, we joined the Free Company of the Mountain Heather, about nine years ago now, but he met a woman in some town or another and decided he might be happier as a goatherd. He wasn't a soldier, not really. Most people can learn to fight. And most young people *want* to, if they care about the war enough. But killing and violence and boredom and trauma take their toll and it's not for everyone. In Hron the same as Vorronia, you'll find most combatants are no older than twenty-five."

"I think I understand," I said. "And I think, by what you're saying, I'm probably no soldier either."

"No shit," Nola said, smiling.

"So the Free Company?" I asked.

"There are about twenty companies skirting around the border of Hron," Nola said. "I joined the Mountain Heather because it watches the pass in from Vorronia. There are about a hundred of us in the Company, but we rotate through, and there are a lot fewer of us active in the winter. Most of the time in the Company, we do nothing but ride and sing and train. We sometimes drive off Vorronian settlers. When I met you, I was coming back from reconnaissance in Tar."

"Do you miss him?" I asked.

"Miss who?"

"Hideon the Imp," I said. "Do you miss him?"

"Not really," Nola said. "He was a sweetheart, but he was a terrible lay. Sorros, on the other hand..."

....

On the third day, us four travelers and Sakana took one of the larger tables in the cafe. "Who did Sorros kill?" I asked Sakana, I suppose forgetting my promise to act tactfully.

"How'd you know that?" she asked. She wasn't mad, however.

"That woman, Marly, called him Ghostmaker, and he called her Ghostmother. He killed her kid?"

Sakana nodded.

"Why? How?"

Sakana smiled sadly. "Have you ever seen Sorros drink?" she asked.

I thought about it. "No, never," I said.

"Sorros doesn't drink," Nola said.

"He used to," Sakana said. "Six years ago, he did something that divided the town in half. I was a teenager then, and my friends and I used to joke that we were going to draw a line down the center of everything and split it into Molik and Nari."

She paused to sip her carsa, then went back to her story. "Sorros was a popular guy, the militia trainer. He taught people firearms, archery, hand-to-hand, strategy, tactics, codes... anything military, he knew it and he taught us. Gently, too. Every other militia representative I've seen since has been kind of... macho I guess. Sorros wasn't like that, except when he was drunk. He was a monster when he was drunk. He had a reputation, and while half the town loved him, the other half started to hate him. Then, one night, Marly's son, his name was Hessol, was drunk in the town square, harassing people. Throwing bottles at people, calling them all kinds of names. He was a grown man acting like a kid, throwing a tantrum. Everyone told him to go home. Two of his friends tried to calm him down, tried to take him away, and he lashed out, shoving them. Sorros came over—they weren't friends, mind you—and knocked him across the face with a baton. Hessol fell on his head and he died two days later as a result of, I don't know the word for it, brain bleeding."

I was quiet.

Nola answered first. "Sounds like an accident," she said.

Sakana nodded. "That's what half of us thought. The other half didn't. No one—well, no one but Marly and a couple of Hessol's friends—wanted to see Sorros dead or packed off to Karak, but a lot of people weren't comfortable with him after that. He was probably the best fighter in town, and instead of just taking Hessol to the ground, he hit him in the face and killed him. Even more than that, he didn't let someone sober handle the problem. So, after the funeral, everyone concerned got together and had a meeting. It went on for two days. Eventually, we agreed—now, I say 'we' even though I wasn't there, but I think they made the right choice. We agreed—Sorros would leave, so Marly and the rest of Hessol's kith and kin wouldn't have to see him every day, and if Sorros wished to show he was sorry, he'd quit drinking."

"If she can't stand him, why did Marly put him up?" I asked.

"She's an odd one, Marly. I think the idea is that if Sorros is going to be here, he should have to *really* feel what he did. She feels her loss every day, so maybe she wants him to understand that, at least for a moment. I assume he's staying in Hessol's old room, sitting at dinner in Hessol's old chair."

"Who would stop him if he didn't want to?" I asked.

Sakana looked at me, considering my question. "You've got strange questions, Borolian. I guess no one. But the reason he's welcome in Moliknari at all is because he's sorry. He shows that by conceding to these sorts of requests. And he shows that he cares about Moliknari itself by having left, by not letting his side turn it into a fight against the other side."

Blosik came to join us at the table.

"You're from Borolia, are you not?" he asked me.

I nodded.

"Do you know why I feed you?"

"I don't," I admitted.

"I feed you because I choose to. In Borolia, you use tokens, yes? By performing tasks, or by being born into wealth, or by controlling other people, you receive tokens, which you leverage against people or trade with people for goods and services?"

"Yeah," I said, "in a manner of speaking. And you don't, here, if I'm right? You simply give out food?"

"I give food to whom I choose," he said. "Some people here will feed you simply for being people. Some people here will feed you because you're militia. I'd probably have fed you once or twice simply for existing, because why not? But I'd feed you much longer because I know you've risked so much, losing your home and almost your arm or your life, on our behalf. But there are other people in this town who wouldn't feed you at all simply because you're friends with Sorros."

"Where do you get your food and tea, then?"

"From farmers. They give it to me because they know I redistribute it fairly. They give it to me because I have a good reputation. In Borolia, you're measured by the tokens you carry, whether you've earned them or not. In Hron, you're measured by your reputation."

"Whether you've earned it or not?" I asked.

"Perhaps," Blosik replied. "Perhaps. But ideally, a reputation is built out of deeds. Like everything in Hron, it is flexible, dynamic. And a reputation might mean different things to different people. There are probably people here who think Hessol had what was coming—I don't, I loved the boy, even if he could be a brat— and to them your friendship with Sorros might be to your honor instead of your discredit."

"What about strangers?" I asked.

"Strangers have a blank slate," he answered. "Myself, I would let strangers drink my carsa for days enough to see what they're made of. If they make themselves useful in some way or another, in my cafe or somewhere else in town, then they're welcome here. If not?" he shrugged. "Then perhaps they should move on."

"So Sorros—" I started.

"If Sorros chose not to stay with Marly, his reception in Moliknari would be very cold indeed."

Ten

An hour before sunset, the first caravan of travelers for Midwinter showed up on skis, a seemingly never-ending procession of families and individuals. Some hauled sledges, others did not. Some brought dogs, others did not. They flooded into town, setting up thick tents and tarps as they went, filling into the empty cracks of streets and buildings.

That night, the guest hall came alive, the rooms filled to capacity with the elderly or sick, with pregnant families, with nursing parents—anyone who needed a warm bed—while others, traveling alone, crowding onto mats on the ground floor. Us four of the Free Company squeezed into one of the smallest rooms and onto two bunk beds. By grace of our injuries, Grem and I were granted the bottom bunks.

As soon as the first guests came to the hall, food preparations began in the generous kitchen alongside the main room. I volunteered to help, but, with no faculty for getting by with only one arm, just got in the way. I retired back to the main room and took a seat at one of the long tables, watching the crowds come in.

It wasn't long before a handsome young man approached and

asked, in a thick Vorronian accent, if he could join me. He was tall and thin, with long black hair and deep-set black eyes, perhaps a year or three older than myself. I'd been too long alone, I thought suddenly.

"Of course," I said, and offered him the seat across from me. He removed his tailed coat, hung it on the chair, then sat. His eyes never left mine.

"I am Charl," he said, his Cer strained almost unintelligible, "recent from Vorronia. This is my first winter in the mountains, and my first festival. And you are?"

"Dimos," I said, in Vorronian, "from Borol."

"Dimos," he repeated. "Your Vorronian is flawless."

"Thank you," I said, smiling.

"As is your smile," he said.

"You're very forward," I responded, but I was still smiling.

We fell to chatting, and he told me his story. He said he was a war refugee, fleeing conscription, that he'd found a home in a town called Mros and joined them to come to the festival, excited to see more of his new country. By the time he was done with his story, we'd been joined by more and more people, young and old, excited from their travels. Dinner came out shortly thereafter, and it was a feast the like of which I'd never seen.

Portioning was done in the kitchen, and each course of the meal came out already on plates. "It's to keep things fair," Dory said, pulling up a chair next to me. "In autumn, we just set the food on the table and let people take as much as they want. In the winter, there's less food, and it's customary for the cooks to dole out portions in the kitchen."

But there was no reason to complain about the serving sizes. We ate buttered beets and sautéed mushrooms, steamed greens and battered squash. There were deep-fried slices of potato and a stew served in bowls of fresh-baked, bitter-herbed bread. Dessert was self-served from copper trays filled with bonbons, cakes, and savory muffins. A few volunteers set up a bar and emptied barrels of mead and beer into flagons.

"Where's the meat?" Charl asked, after the last plate had been served.

"A lot of Hron is vegetarian," Dory replied. "At festivals, we don't serve meat at the banquets."

"The meat makes the man," Charl replied, indignant and rude. I began to reconsider my crush, and I began to understand why so many Hronish people I'd met had been reluctant to befriend a foreigner. But as I fell further into my cups, Charl regained his charm. He regaled us all with tales of adventure in Vorronia, of his times at sea on merchantmen, of his daring, solo flight into the mountains with the Borolian press gang on his trail.

Finally, drunker than I'd been in months, I stood up and announced my intention to sleep. I gripped the back of my chair to steady myself.

"Do you want company?" Charl asked.

I thought about it. I wanted it. "I'm too drunk, I think," I said, my brain confused at what my mouth chose to say. "I'll see you tomorrow, though?"

"It would be my pleasure," he said, then went back to the conversation at the table.

I stumbled to bed, lay on my back, and slept happy.

....

Obviously, alcohol only has the effect of borrowing happiness from the future, and waking up was harder on my body than I would have liked. But soldier habits—even those newly formed—die hard, and I couldn't manage to sleep much past dawn, so I woke with an aching head and shoulder. Carsa and leftover potatoes were waiting in the kitchen, so that helped. And for a moment, when I was lost in my self-loathing for having caused my own hangover, I remembered that roughly a week prior I had been shot in the arm in the heat of battle—suddenly, a hangover seemed a pittance of a problem.

Sakana was in the kitchen, along with ten or so volunteers, cleaning the place.

"I'd like to help," I said, while sipping carsa with my good hand.

"I'd like you to too," she said, though I knew by then she was only teasing. "But you've got a genuine war wound and can't really do much good."

"There's a lot of not much good I'm doing," I said.

Sakana put down her scouring pad and walked up to me. "It's fine. When I told you about everyone pulling their own weight, I think I might have glossed over the part where we help each other out."

"Yeah, okay," I said, not quite convinced.

"Let me show you around the festival," she said. "You'll barely recognize Moliknari from yesterday." She hooked her arm through mine and we left the hall.

The city was indeed transformed. Bright banners hung from rooftops and an entire shantytown had been built overnight, leaving only narrow walkways through the streets. People snored on cots and on the pavement under heavy furs and wool, and the smells of barley grits and spiced meat filled the air as others began to cook breakfast.

The central square was mostly free of squatters. In the middle was a block of ice the size of a house, with scaffolding up its side and at least a dozen workers crawling over the thing with chisel and hammer, carving it into something.

"The town's population more than doubles when we host a festival," Sakana said, leading me past a makeshift ball court. Children from five to ten, bundled up for the weather, were playing some game that seemed to involve hitting one another in the head with a comically-large hollow leather ball.

"These people are from all over Hron?" I asked.

"In a summer festival, absolutely. A midwinter festival only attracts maybe a third the travelers a summer one will—most of these folks traveled less than a week to reach us. There are, I think, three midwinter festivals happening this year, spread out across the country."

"What are they for?"

"*Frenna*," Sakana replied.

"What's that?"

"You'll see.

....

The short day went fast, spent as it was sitting on the brazier-and-brick heated porch of the cafe with my friends. Sorros joined us that morning, and he was uncharacteristically quiet. One look from Nola, and I knew better than to ask him how his days had been. We drank *frenna*, a low alcohol, spiced beer that was apparently brewed just for festivals and other such occasions.

"They key to a good festival is maintaining your drunkenness somewhere a little below 'stupor' until late into the night," Grem said, when he came to join us at lunch.

"I prefer 'not at all,' personally," Nola said, turning to refill her mug of carsa from a samovar on the table behind them.

While her back was turned, Grem stuck his tongue out at her, his eyes crossed, his fingers in his ears, in an uncharacteristic display. "I've been sober this whole damn war," he said, when she turned back around. "I mean to spend today very close to unreasonably drunk."

The conversation lapsed and I returned to watching the street. When I'd been riding with the imperial army, I hadn't really learned to distinguish the people of one town from the next. But after my time with the Free Company, and a few days in Moliknari, I think I started to recognize how differently people dressed and acted.

Men and women from Moliknari favored ponchos instead of cloaks, and a lot of the strangers wore skirts instead of pants. The color schemes and the patterns were all different, and I was fairly certain that if I spent enough time in the mountains, I'd learn to tell where people were from by whether their cloaks were floral or abstract, earth tone or pastel. Others wore what I assumed to be festival garments, from tight-fitted single garments like union suits to ostrich-feather-ornamented vests paired with skirts worn with leggings. On a very few, the style seemed distinctly Vorronian—tight-fitting pants and shirts in blacks and grays, with wide-brimmed felted flat-top bowlers or other Imperial-style hats.

"Hey, where do I get clothes like that?" I asked Sorros, nodding to a young man dressed in such garb.

"Hronople," he said. "Looks good, but it's not practical."

The young man saw us looking and walked towards us. His hair was long with black ringlets that framed a handsome angular face, and his eyes were dark and piercing.

"I'd love something to drink," he said. "Do you mind if I join you?"

"Not at all," Sakana and I said at the same time. He pulled a chair up next to Sakana and introduced himself to us as Varin, giving a polite but joking one-fist salute to those of us in militia garb and offering a loose handshake to the others. Then, when he sat down, he pulled out a pouch of what I presumed to be tobacco and rolled a cigarette. He offered it around the table, and while my friends dismissed the offer, I accepted and he lit the cigarette.

I breathed in. It wasn't tobacco.

"What is this?" I asked.

"Mugwort," he said.

"What does it do?"

Dory and Sorros started laughing.

"Nothing," Sorros said.

"It's good for your stomach, good for your dreams," Varin said.

"You're talking to a man who smokes opium and tobacco," Sorros said. "And by comparison, yeah. Mugwort does nothing."

It tasted okay, but yeah, it did nothing. I took out my pouch and lit a pipe of tobacco, then offered it to Varin.

"What brings you from Hronople?" Sakana asked him.

"I've been on the road six months," he answered. "Journeyman."

"Oh?" Blosik inquired, "what trade?"

"Writer's guild," he answered, then started coughing on the smoke.

"Two useless bastards at one table, then!" Blosik shouted, slightly drunk and clearly happy. "Our Mr. Horacki was a journalist out of Borol before he fell in with and saved the Free Company of the Mountain Heather."

I expected Varin to bristle—I would have bristled at such high praise aimed at another writer upon first introductions—but instead he turned to me and beamed.

"I want to know everything about your mother country" he said, in thickly-accented Boroli.

"I'd be happy to tell you," I said, in Cer to keep the conversation from drifting away from those at the table who weren't fluent in my first language.

"I've been working on a story set in one of your... *prisons*..." he said, using the unfamiliar Vorronian word, "and I want to know everything."

"I haven't been in a cell since I was little," I answered.

"They put *children* in prison?"

"No," I said. "Well, yes. It's a different prison and we don't use the word prison, we call it a reformatory. For children who misbehave."

"What's the difference between a reformatory and a prison?" he asked. He pulled out a notebook and began to take down my words.

"A reformatory has the ostensible purpose of reforming young offenders, so that they won't commit further crimes upon their release."

"And a prison doesn't?"

"It... well, that's the ostensible purpose of prisons too, but society doesn't bother as hard with that facade. The recidivism rate in both is incredibly high, however. Most imperial advisors seem to think that the solution to this problem is longer sentences, to scare away potential criminals and to keep those who do commit crimes away from the rest of society."

"Does it work?" the young man asked.

"It's a crime against humanity!" Sorros yelled. "They put humans in cages and they call it justice. They keep them away from light, from company, from anything that might possibly help them come to understand the need for social behavior, then put them *back* in cages, for *longer*, when they act out!"

"Hear, hear," Blosik said.

"What would you have us do with criminals, then?" I asked.

"Give them medals," Sorros said. "For daring to be antisocial in the face of an antisocial order."

Varin replied more calmly. "From what little I understand of it—which I assure you, is little indeed—your system seeks to 'punish' a class of people it deems 'criminal.' That's not the way we work. If a crime has been committed, like theft, assault, murder, or rape, we take each instance as its own unique event. What's the most common crime in Borol? What are most of the people in your prisons guilty of?"

"Theft," I answered. "Or assault or murder related to theft." I'd been arrested for theft a half-dozen times myself.

"We don't have that here," Varin said.

"Bullshit," I replied. "You have people? And people own things? You have theft."

"We mostly don't, actually," Nola said. "In Vorronia, we had theft. In Hron, it's one of the rarest crimes. I think that in general, people steal things that they need, or occasionally things that they want. People steal food, or they steal expensive things to sell to buy food. In Hron, food is free. Shelter is free. Nothing is 'expensive,' because nothing is bought or sold or bartered. Theft is usually a crime of poverty, and here there's no poverty."

"Most thieves in this country are children," Varin explained, "stealing to be mean, to deprive someone else of something. But they learn the social cost of that pretty quickly, when no one'll play with them. And, yeah, sometimes adults steal things of sentimental or practical value. Like with any other crime, if they're caught, or they own up to it, they face the consequences of their actions."

"Which are?" I asked.

"If what you did isn't a big deal, you might lose some of your friends over it, or just deal with everyone being mad at you. If it's something major, you might not be welcome where you're from, and it's likely that those hurt by your actions will ask a few specific things of you—like what happened to Sorros. And the truly unrepentant?" Varin emptied his mug of frenna, then continued. "They can fuck off. If they're clearly a danger, like an unrepentant rapist or murderer, then we'll probably kill them. If they aren't, if they're just an asshole who doesn't want to act socially with others, then they can go to Karak or out into the rest of the world."

"Karak," I said. "Is that your prison?"

"No," Nola said. "Karak is a hellish place but it's a hellish place of its residents' own making. It's a town of the antisocial. It's still better than Vorronia, if you ask me—there's no king, no conscription, no prison, law, or money. But it's full of people too proud to apologize, who'd rather fight someone than talk things out, who don't care how their actions affect their neighbors."

"Does it work?" I asked, "does holding people accountable without trial work? Have you ever killed the wrong person? Ostracized someone who didn't deserve it? Is the threat of social stigma enough to keep you safe?"

"It kept us safe until the Borolian empire decided to march on our villages and burn them," Sorros said.

"Does prison work?" Varin asked.

"No," I admitted.

"The Hronish system isn't perfect," Nola said. "But it's a hell of a lot better than anything else I've seen."

"Fair," I said. "And if I can say nothing else about your fine country, I'm quite fond of the prices."

This was good for a laugh from the drunker of my companions, and Varin offered a toast to Hron.

....

The festival began at sundown, with all the assembled towns-folk and visitors crowding into the central square. Our party sat nearby on the roof of the guest hall, on a series of aged wooden bleachers that slotted into notches set into the tiles. Below us, the massive severed head of a giant, carved from ice, lay on its side on the cobbles. Its tongue was hanging from its mouth of pitted and twisted teeth, the eyes were squinted in death. A woman dressed in a snow-white poncho and skirt stood in front of the sculpture and bellowed, though the acoustics weren't good enough for her voice to carry to where we sat.

"What's she saying?" Varin asked.

"The head is Lord Winter," Sakana answered. "One of the titans."

The woman raised the pitch of her voice into song, a slow operatic tone. Torchbearers strode down the aisles of the crowd, lighting iron braziers as they went, filling the air with tangy smoke. They reached the singer, went around her, and set their torches to the head of ice. The flame snaked up the side, following the trail of some accelerant, then lit pools of liquid fuel set into the sculpture's eyes, mouth, and crown.

The woman finished her song and the crowd roared.

....

"The first night is ceremony and drinking," Sakana said, as she led Varin and I into the crowd. "The second night is games and drinking, the third night is cleanup and drinking. The fourth day we call *gorasi*, which some people might tell you is the old word for 'rest' but it really means 'hangover.'"

"Gorasi is my favorite day of it," Varin said. "You don't really know someone until you see them recover from a festival."

"If I drink this much every day," I said, "I'll never make it to gorasi."

"Most everyone switches to water at midnight," Sakana said.

The music started, a sort of crowd-song. Sakana and Varin knew their parts and stood arm in arm belting out the words to some fantastical opera, while all around me the square began to become one complex, multi-throated voice. Curious, I left them to explore. Some people played instruments, and the song itself changed tone and character as I wove through the crowd: more ethereal here where flutes and baritones dominated, more crass and throaty where horns and drunks prevailed. The incense from the braziers continued to burn, and people in white moved through the crowd with food and drink.

I found a seat on a bench from which to people watch and eavesdrop. A strange hobby, maybe, but one that has done me plenty of good as a writer. Nearby, a trio of happy, gray-haired locals were arguing, loudly to hear one another over the crowd song.

"It's better this way," one of them, clearly the oldest, said. She had a necklace of teeth that, I was guessing, marked her as a widow.

"Too many people from out of town," a man said. By his tone, I assumed him to be the sort who enjoyed his role as a curmudgeon. "I wouldn't want to bet that one in three of people here know the sagas, know why we burn the ice titan."

"I'm not sure one in three of my own grandchildren know the

sagas, and they're Moliknari born and raised," the third said, her gray hair tied in a braided crown.

"There's the problem," the man said. "The accord. Before we were Hron we knew where we were *from*, by the Mountain, and we knew what that made us."

"Lonely and bored," the first woman said, "from what I recall. I met my Gorry at the first festival we ever hosted for our neighbors, and there's not a chance I would have without the accord."

"Bah. Before the accord we cared about *tradition*," the man continued. He accented the word tradition with a subconscious toast of his mug and downed more of whatever he was drinking.

"What's this, then," the first woman said, "besides our tradition? We've burned the titan to make way for spring and it doesn't ruin it for me that some folks from Holl are here."

Charl approached my bench, interrupting my eavesdropping. "Mind if I sit?" he asked.

"Please," I said.

"I don't get any of this," he said.

"I don't either," I replied, "but I'm having a good time."

He laughed and I think I swooned a little. Certainly, if I had the coloration to blush I would have done so.

"Are you drunk?" he asked.

"The tiniest bit," I said, "but not so much. This frenna is good stuff."

"Then, if you'd permit me, we could go somewhere more private? We can wait until you're sober and see how you feel?"

He put his hand on my leg. I reached out and held it. He smiled, I smiled.

And ten minutes later, on the roof of the guest hall, he tried to murder me.

Eleven

We were alone on the bleachers when he pulled the knife on me.

"Rat bastard!" he yelled, then lunged.

I had my brass knuckles on in an instant. I don't even remember going into my bag, I just remember having them out. Gunfights were new and frightening, but a knife fight was something I understood. I put out my arm, my bad arm, and he went for it. Even trained knife fighters seem to go for what's closest. I pulled back my arm and got him in the sternum with my other fist, knocking him back.

"Help," I yelled. "Help!"

I moved in towards him and he pulled a gun. Not fair. Distantly, I heard my call for help echoed down below.

"I know you," I said, "don't I? You were with the army."

He cocked the gun. I leapt to the side as he fired and I slammed my good shoulder into the wooden bench.

He screamed in anger, turning to aim again.

I twisted away as a bullet shattered the wood where I'd been. I found my feet and dove for the gun before he could pull back the hammer to fire again. We wrestled on the roof as I continued to cry out.

While the assassin and I tousled on the roof, footsteps rushed up the stairs. I was no match for the fellow, though. He had military training and I had a bullet wound.

"Get off of him!" I heard an old woman yell, then a boot was kicking Charl in the ribs with a fierce determination.

Charl pulled off of me and stood. I scrambled to my knees and saw that the three people I'd been eavesdropping on had joined me on the roof. The younger of the two woman—still easily in her late fifties—had been kicking my attacker and stood brandishing a ceramic mug.

"Back the fuck off, old woman!" Charl screamed. "I have a gun!"

"I can see that," she said, then stepped in swinging.

He fired and my heart leapt. The bullet struck the woman in the forearm, and I can't swear to it but I think I heard her bone shatter from where I was. I grappled Charl by the legs while the woman's friends came in and disarmed my attacker.

The gray-haired man turned to the fallen woman and helped raise her wounded arm over her heart. A dozen more people piled up the stairs and one took over treatment, ordering one person to keep back the crowd, another to bring him supplies, a third to assist him as he fashioned a tourniquet from his own shirt. People obeyed.

The oldest woman took the man's gun and looked to me.

"Who is he?" she asked.

"An assassin," I said, gasping for breath. "Sent to kill me. The Borolians."

"Who are you?" she asked.

"Dimos," I said. "A journalist. Of the Free Company of the Mountain Heather."

The woman turned to her captive, put the gun to his chest, winced, then fired. She cocked the gun back and fired into his dead body until the bullets were spent. She had one hand over her face but peered through the cracks in her fingers.

"Why'd you help me?" I asked, once I'd found myself sitting on the bleacher with my three saviors. "He had a gun. He could have killed you."

"You must be new here," the old man said. "This is Hron."

....

Later, I found Nola. "When I was on the roof, a man was treating the woman's gunshot wound," I said. "He ordered people around like a military commander, and everyone obeyed. So you *do* use authority here?"

Nola thought about it for a minute before answering. "We do, yes. We allow, in some circumstances, people with the authority of experience to control things. And there's nothing un-free about it. One of the best feelings in the world is letting someone else take charge of you for moments, when you do so willingly. Sometimes, the things that are the worst when they happen to you without your consent are the best things when they happen to you *with* your consent. Touching, sex, restraint, command. Fighting. Confession. Conversation. Responsibility. Choosing to do things is all the difference in the world."

....

I slept badly that night, and was glad that, when I woke from nightmares, I was in a room with my friends. Sorros had moved out from Marly's house and he and Nola were curled up together in the bunk above me, both snoring softly.

I stared at the moonlight on the floor for what must have been an hour. I scarcely remembered who I had been when I'd donned a mask to creep through the trees with the Free Company before that battle, and the novelty and excitement of the war had long since been lost on me. I was exhausted and jumpy, and worse than that, I was hunted. I missed my apartment and the relative safety of the near-poverty I'd left.

The next morning, at breakfast, those of us of the Free Company talked over our options.

"We can't stay here," I said, and no one disagreed.

"We move on to Holl," Nola said, "and from there it's only five days to Hronople. Once we're in the city, we can call for a council of war.

"We should get on our way then," Dory said.

"Right now?" Sorros asked, casting a mournful gaze to the food in front of us that we would be leaving.

"I've been telling people to meet in the square after lunch," Nola said. "They want to hear war stories, but unfortunately, instead, we're going to tell them stories of the coming war."

....

"Now I know you don't like me much," Sorros began, from where he stood at the center of the square, in the spot so recently occupied by the head of Lord Winter. The square was almost as crowded as it had been during the evening's ceremonies, and the same white-dressed figures moved through the crowd with food and drink.

"We like Borolia even less," someone shouted, and was met with laughter.

Nola stepped forward. She'd never looked so tall or powerful as she did that day, dressed in freshly-laundered militia garb. When the General spoke, people listened.

"The army came in and struck the smallest villages, taking their birds and winter stores like common bandits," she said. "They killed suspected militants, and when Sotoris put up a fight, they burned it to the ground."

People murmured at that.

"The men who did that are dead." In Cer, the word "men" doesn't connote all of humanity the way it does in some other languages, so her choice of calling the soldiers "men" was one that put emphasis on their gender. "The Free Company of the Mountain Heather ambushed and killed them."

That was good for a long, sustained cheer.

"We wouldn't be alive, let alone victorious, without the help of Dimos Horacki," Nola continued, "a journalist who saw injustice and knew it for what it was, a man who fled from our enemies and came over to us." I decided not to correct her on the fine point of whether or not I had fled or simply survived. "And he's got, well, unpleasant news. Please, my friends, my comrades, heed his words."

I stepped forward. I don't know for certain why I wasn't nervous about speaking in a foreign tongue before so many strangers. Perhaps, as I like to think, I was born for the stage. Most likely, I was still in shock from the previous night's attempt on my life and to be honest my only concern as to the size of the crowd was that it might hold in its numbers another assassin. But people were on the lookout for such behavior and any would-be murderer would be unlikely to survive an attempt on my life.

"We killed Dolan Wilder, General Armsman of His Majesty's Imperial Army, and killed or routed his men. This is a huge blow against the Borolian propaganda machine—they'd put a lot stock in Wilder, and his death isn't going to be taken lightly." Tried as I might, my voice didn't carry with the power of Nola's, and I paused occasionally to allow those who could understand to relay what I said to those who couldn't.

"They came into the Cerracs to tame a savage people," I said. "To mine your mountains for coal and iron. They didn't expect resistance. But they'll be back, and stronger. A hundred times stronger."

"How soon?" someone asked.

"I don't know. Spring, most likely. Summer, if they want to be careful."

"How many?"

We'd talked about this all morning, and decided, to Nola's displeasure, to tell them the truth. She had been convinced that the truth would inspire only despair. Sorros, however, insisted that the whole of the truth was essential so that people could make informed decisions, could truly be autonomous. "He commands thirty thousand men," I announced. "By summer, he could have four times that many, trained soldiers all."

Nothing I have said in my life has caused more fear in more people than those two sentences. Some shook their heads, cast their gazes to the ground. Others looked around, as though the army was upon them already.

"We're fucked!" a kid from the crowd yelled.

"We're not fucked," Grem said, walking to the fore of the stage, supported by his sister. "If you tell me you think we're fucked then you're saying I lost my friends for nothing."

"We're fucked," the kid yelled. "Fuck your friends, fuck your leg, we're all going that way soon enough."

"To hell with that!" Dory shouted. Most of the murmuring stopped. I'll never understand how some people command attention and others don't. "How many Borolians know these mountains? How many of them know the canyons? How many imperial soldiers do you think can tell the difference between a rocky trail and a dammed up river that's waiting to drown them? We're fighting for Hron, gods dammit, and they're fighting for little tokens that they keep in their pocket to spend on sex and food."

Nola spoke next. "We can win. I'm not saying we *will*, I'm saying we *can*. We can win this war if we start accepting that it's coming *now*. We need to raise and train militias, manufacture arms, set up posts and ambush points, fortify and booby trap our towns, everything. We need everyone to start scheming, and more than that, start working. In one month's time, there's going to be a council of war in Hronople. Every town, smallholding, and militia should send their spokespersons so we can share our plans, needs, and what we know."

I'm rarely tempted as a journalist to lie in print, but I truly wish I could write here that the crowd was jubilant, that we had rallied their spirits and sent them off with a renewed sense of hope. But of course, we didn't. Our tidings were grim, and as much as we tried to cheerlead, we left no one in a spirited mood.

After the rally, we got ready to go. We'd head to Holl, then Hronople. Grem and Dory chose to accompany us to the city, in part to be extra sets of eyes and arms in case of attack en route, in part so that Grem might see a prosthetist.

"You're not the bastard I thought you were," Sakana said to me as she helped me pack my effects.

"Thanks," I said.

"No, I mean it. And more than that, I'm sorry how I was the first day."

"I'd already forgotten," I said. "And thanks, sincerely, for the hospitality."

Sakana grinned. "I'll be getting plenty of it myself. Hospitality, that is. I'm leaving with Varin. You inspired us, we're going to spread the word. 'Make plans for war, and send a spokes to the council.' Varin thinks we can hit six, maybe seven towns and still make it in time for the council ourselves. There's a meeting tomorrow after lunch for those of us who're going to be messengers, so we can be sure to make it everywhere."

"I can't wait to see you in Hronople," I said.

I signed the log in the guest hall, going on perhaps at overdue length—the writer's curse—about how pleasant I'd found my stay.

Sammit and Dammit were relieved to see us when we picked them up from the dog run on our way out of the city, and the houndswoman who'd been keeping them seemed relieved to see them go. "These aren't town dogs," I believe her words were. "Lovable I'm sure, but get them the hell out of here."

I remember that encounter more vividly than some of the other more mundane encounters I've had in Hron, because I remember it was when it occurred to me that this gruff, grumpy demeanor seemed endemic to the country. A curious thing for a group of people who share freely and keep no track of debt or wealth.

Then we were off, and I remembered just how goddam much it hurt to ride a horse with a bullet wound in your arm.

Twelve

"Does this hurt?" Nola asked when she washed the bullet hole.

"Yes, goddammit," I replied. "It hurts like shit!"

"I'm sorry," she said. "I'm going to pour alcohol on the wound now. Are you going to punch me when I do it?"

"I don't know," I said. I was drunk. "Probably."

"I'm not going to do it if you're going to punch me," Nola said.

"I'll try not to punch you."

She poured alcohol on the wound. I've got nothing to compare the pain to. Fortunately, I was drunk. I didn't even punch her.

"Can I pass out now?" I asked.

"Not yet," she answered. "Not until I've got this new bandage on."

She took the freshly-boiled bandage from where it sat in a pot of medicinal tea, then wrapped it around my arm. It hurt, but it hurt so much less than the alcohol that the pain scarcely even registered.

"Now you can pass out," she said. "Just don't go falling into the mud again while wrestling a dog."

"Yes, General," I said, then I passed out.

....

We stopped for the night at a smallholding—one of the hundreds or thousands of small homesteads scattered across the country. Most were farms or artisan lodges. This ones, Sorros explained on our approach, was a library.

Dogs barked at our arrival, and a giant of a man strode out the door and showed us to the stables.

When he saw Sorros, he bear hugged him and lifted him two feet off the ground. Then he clasped each of our hands in turn as we were introduced.

"This is Mol," Sorros said. I've plenty of practice learning foreign tongues, but it took me three tries to pronounce his name to his satisfaction.

"A friend of Sorros is a friend of mine," he said, then led us into the house.

It was as warm as summer inside, and we stripped down to our long underwear in the front room.

The house was a single story, half built of glass, and sprawling. Every wall that wasn't a window was a bookshelf, and I saw books in at least eight languages. It was warm and there were books. I wasn't sure I ever wanted to leave.

The "kitchen" was a counter in the living room, and we fell back into comfortable chairs while Mol returned to the stew. A fat, happy black cat was on my lap in an instant.

"So what is it you do here?" I asked.

"Careful," Sorros said, "Dimos here is a journalist."

Mol laughed politely, then answered me. "Me, I make glass. My wife Somi—she's in the city, hates the winter—she's a tactical historian."

Dory and Nola both perked up.

"All these books—" Dory started.

"Military history, tactical theory. Analysis of battles."

"Can we—" Dory asked.

"Nothing that looks older than, I don't know, a hundred years," Mol said. "And Somi will kill me if you damage anything. But other than that, go ahead."

Dory and Nola looked at each other like children, then got up and began to explore.

"Tell Dimos why you live here," Sorros said. "Tell him how you heat your house."

"Thermal vents," Mol said. "The whole house is set over a crevasse in the earth."

"You live on a volcano?" I asked. "I'm sitting on top of a volcano?"

"Not on top of," Mol said. "At the base of. And yes. One day his whole place will go up in flames or be buried under molten rock. But in the meantime, my house is warm and I've got the furnace of my dreams."

"Mol supplies half of western Hron's windows," Sorros said. I'd never seen him so proud of anyone.

"How does that work?" I asked.

"Well, so I'm not part of any specific town," Mol said, "but it works not too different than if I was. Towns and smallholdings send things around—trade, if you will—just like people within a town do. I can head into Holl and pick up supplies and they know they're welcome here to pick up glass anytime they need. I grow and hunt about half of what I eat out here, and I get grains in town. But people only need windows every now and then, and I need food every day. So it can't work one-for-one. It's not barter."

"I get that," I said. "But what if there's famine? Is a farmer in Holl really going to set aside grains for you when there's barely enough to go around? Or if half the country has a drought, can they make the other half feed them?"

"Make?" Mol said. "No. And it's come to that a few times. A hard year, you'll really learn who your friends are."

I thought back to my years in the boarding house, and more so, my time on the streets. "Sharing is easy when there's enough to go around. It gets harder when you're hungry."

"I've never heard truer words," Mol said. "We've had some bad years. But as much as adversity can drive people apart, set people to hoarding, it can bring out the best in people. When it comes down to it, we all agree—if there's not enough to go around, Hron will share with Hron. It's hard and it's awful and we do it."

"Is that part of the accord?"

Mol laughed. "I have no idea. I think so?"

"This is how Karak got asked to leave Hron," Sorros said.

"Pardon?" I asked.

"We expect a culture to abide by the accord the same as we expect people to. If a culture doesn't want to share, that's fine, that's on them, but the rest of us want to be with people who do. Karak was just a smallholding at the very south-eastern edge of Hron when the accord got signed, and they opened their doors to anyone who wanted a taste of 'real freedom.' Five years later, the whole west and north of the country lost its harvest, and everyone pitched in. Everyone but Karak. They want to live alone? Let them."

"I can see why you don't like them," I said.

"Here's to Hron, then," Mol said, serving out bowls of stew. "Greens from the greenhouse, grains from the foothills, and guests from half the continent."

We lifted our bowls in a makeshift toast and then ate. Travel does wonders for the appetite.

After dinner, Nola and Sorros slipped out to walk in the moonlight, and the rest of us stayed up late talking. Grem was feeling lively, and I saw hints of his old self peering out through the gloom.

"How's the leg?" I asked.

"Lack of leg," he answered, but he was smiling.

"How's the lack of leg?" I asked.

"It's amazing," he said. "It doesn't hurt all the time anymore."

"I've still got your concertina," I said.

"It's too soon," Grem answered. "I'll get back to it one day but not yet."

"Hey Mol," Dory said, "you've known Sorros for awhile, yeah?"

"I have," Mol answered.

"Tell us an embarrassing story about him."

Mol stared at his beer for awhile, thinking.

"Sorros Ralm. We grew up together in Moliknari. He went off to join the Free Companies and I went off to make glass."

"You were friends since you were kids?" Dory asked.

"Hell no, I couldn't stand him," Mol said. "If I've ever met a man who hated work, it's him. I swear on the Mountain I'm pretty sure he joined the militia because he'd rather get shot at than work hard. And he only did *that* because half the town was threatening to cut him off if he didn't do *something*. So here's your embarrassing story: when we were, I don't know, fourteen or something, we had the summer festival, and Sorros decided that frenna wasn't enough, he wanted liquor. Darkness fell at last and we gathered in the square. The summer song began. My friends and I went to unveil the maple titan, tore off the sheets. And there was young Mr. Ralm, curled up naked and snoring, in the crown. We startled him awake and he jumped to his feet, then threw up on the chanter."

Dory had started giggling halfway into the story, then broke out into full-on fits of laughter by the end.

"So what happened?" I asked.

"We got him down, hosed him off, and the crowd chopped up the titan while singing the hymn of summer."

"No," I meant, "what happened with you and Sorros? You're close now?"

"Ah," Mol said. "That's a better story. At least a nicer one. A year after the uh, the incident in Moliknari... not the naked and drunk incident, the killing someone incident... Sorros came here to study with Somi. He was here the whole winter, and they really fell for each other."

"That must have been hard," I said.

"Saved my marriage," Mol said. "Yeah, it was kind of hard at the time, but it wasn't too bad. He was really sweet to her and me both, and we talked it all out. Her and I'd been married two years and the spark was already fading. Sorros steps in for a few months, and suddenly it's back. She was feeling smothered and she didn't even know it. Ever since, she winters in Hronople, and we're stronger than we've ever been."

"Is that common here?"

"Open relationships?" Mol asked. "It's common enough. Maybe not the norm. It's funny, all these years later, to see Sorros and Nola... there's no one else in the world for either of them, from what I gather."

"Everyone's got to find what works for them, I guess," I said.

Mol lifted his glass and drank, then stared out the window behind me and smiled.

I turned, and Sorros and Nola were standing in the yard, lit by the moon, hand in hand.

. . . .

We rode into Holl the next afternoon and, for the first time in all my travels, there was no significant gathering waiting for us in the town square.

"Where is everyone?" I asked. We'd passed a few herders out with their flocks in the fields, but the town looked practically abandoned.

"Inside, I'd guess," Sorros said. "It's winter. A quarter of the town probably went to the festival and won't be back for a few days, and the rest are likely at home, enjoying the warmth of a wood-burning stove."

Once I'd acclimated to the country, I began to realize just how different every town was from its neighbors. The general building style was dictated by available construction materials and weather conditions, but each settlement had its own flair. In Holl, the stonework was astounding, and most buildings bore gargoyles and ornaments a thousand years old.

We rode to the guest hall and stabled our horses. The stable was remarkably warm, as it was built as a sort of greenhouse—the southern wall, facing the winter sun, was a skeletal frame filled with thick glass panes while the northern wall buried into the side of the hill for insulation. We left Sammit and Dammit there as well and strode into the hall proper, which was sadly less well heated than the stables.

By the fire, a young woman in a wheelchair and a man in a large cushioned chair looked up from their respective books at the newcomers.

"Can I help you?" the woman asked. By her voice, I suspected she had a mental, as well as physical, impairment.

"We're from the Free Company of the Mountain Heather," Nola said. "We're heading to Hronople, calling for a council of war. If possible, we'd like to call a council here in Holl, as well."

The young man walked up to us and nodded, then put on his cloak, summoned Nola with a gesture, and the two of them strode out the door.

....

The next morning, I smoked the last of my tobacco as the sun rose over the mountains.

"Where can I get more tobacco?" I asked.

"You can't," Sorros said. "Not in Hron."

I got angry. "You banned tobacco?"

"No," Sorros said. "It doesn't grow here."

"You don't trade with anyone, is that the idea?"

"We don't have any system in place for trade," Sorros said. "We exchange goods through mutual aid. Until we find another anarchist country, I don't think we'll be trading."

"That's absurd," I said. I'd finally found something I disliked about Hron. "Countries don't trade with other countries because they've got some deep love for their neighbors. They do it because it enriches life, provides variety, allows progress—"

"Don't care," Sorros said.

I fumed.

....

"We mostly make our decisions independently, as individuals or small groups," Grem explained, as I walked with him and Dory through the city street on the way to the council. "In order to make sure that what we're doing doesn't step on one another's toes, we have council meetings. They're mostly for coordination, for information sharing, like this one we called for in Hronople. But sometimes we have to make decisions as a town, so we bring it up at council. Every town does it differently. In Sotoris we had it once a week, or more often in emergencies. Everyone who wants to comes and we talk everything through. It's boring as hell."

"Give me an example," I said. "Not of how boring they are, but what you talk about."

"Let's say I want to build a house, right? That's pretty much my business, but I suppose there are things about it that might affect other people, like if I put it where it steals the sun from another building. So I should probably bring it up at council, let everyone know what I'm planning to do. If someone has objections, they'll bring them up and we can work it out."

"So what are things you all have to decide together?" I asked.

"You know, they're actually pretty rare. Even if I wanted to like, change the name of the town, let's say from Sotoris to Gremshold. There's not really an 'official' name for the town anyway, a name is just the thing we all more-or-less agree to call something. So I wouldn't put it to the council, I'd just start calling it Gremshold and see if it took off."

"I'll call it Gremshold," I said.

"Yeah, sure, just don't burn it down again." He was smiling. "Okay, here's an example that happened here in Holl. Ten years ago, everyone was getting sick. Some people looked into it, and it was the shit. The old pit toilets were full. A handful of people worked out the actual details of how to get a sewage system in place, but they couldn't exactly go into people's houses and install these better toilets without clearing it with everyone, so they took it to the council. It wasn't hard to convince people though. The system they designed, with worms to process the waste, has since been put in place in like half of Hron."

"So the council is your system of government?"

"I bet you're sick of hearing this answer from everyone," Grem said, "but... yes and no. Mostly no. It can only make decisions for itself and for the people who choose to abide by its decisions, which is most of us most of the time. If the council agreed to something I didn't, because, let's say, I wasn't there because going to council is dull as shit, I don't really have to abide by it. But then again, I get a hell of a lot out of being part of society, and if I want to continue to do so, I probably am going to have to abide by most of the council's decisions."

"I don't think council is dull," Dory said. It was the first time she'd spoken on the walk.

"You wouldn't," Grem said. "You're old."

We reached the council building, a stone pavilion with heavy tarps hung over the sides for winter, and walked in. Maybe two hundred people were gathered—nearly a third of the town's population, sitting on stepped benches in a circle, drinking tea and carsa and liquor from stoneware goblets. The three of us found seats at the top, next to Sorros and the two guest hall caretakers, and listened.

At the center and bottom of the circle, Nola stood next to a middle-aged gentleman who seemed to be running the meeting.

"We'll hear from our guests," the man said.

"Thank you," Nola said.

"Where are you from?" someone interrupted, once they heard her accent.

"I hardly see how that matters," someone else responded.

"I'm from Vorronia," Nola said. "And I can see how where I'm from might play into your decisions. I've lived in Hron for ten years now, and most of those I've spent guarding the borders with the Free Company of the Mountain Heather."

"I can vouch for that," one woman in the crowd said.

"As can I," said another voice.

"I'll ask that anyone who has questions about the reputation of our guests please inquire shortly after the council," the facilitator said. "Please, Nola, continue."

Nola gave a similar speech as she had at Moliknari, with similar results. When called upon, I walked down to the center and said what I suspected about the invading force, then returned to my seat. After speaking her followup piece, Nola came and sat with us.

"So then, a council of war has been called in Hronople and we've been asked to ready ourselves for invasion," the facilitator said. "Do we want to brainstorm in this group now? Or set this question of how we defend ourselves to smaller groups and individuals, then return to discuss this in the near future, perhaps tomorrow?"

"Those who would like to could stay here to discuss it as a town," one person recommended, "but also know that we'll meet about it again tomorrow, and those who'd prefer to think this through on their own or in smaller groups would be free to do so?"

"Agreed," a voice shouted.

"Objections? Counter-proposals?" the facilitator asked.

There were none, and while some of the people left the pavilion, presumably to discuss plans elsewhere, most stayed and talked for hours. The facilitator kept his opinions to himself and simply helped the discussion stay on the various trains of thought it explored, keeping track of tangents to return to later. I was as astounded by the process as I was by the discussion. There was almost no desperation in the council, what's more, unlike at the talk we had given in Moliknari. What I came to realize is that by coming to people in Holl as we did, to their council, we had simply given them information and empowered them to find the solutions to their problems. Rather than shouting to them as a crowd, as a mass, we spoke to them as peers and appealed to their collective wisdom to find solutions to the problems we presented.

For the first time in weeks, I had hope. I had hope, a hot shower, and warm food, and the doctor who came to the guest hall to check on me seemed to think the worst was through. Just no tobacco.

Once I realized that I was happy, however, I got scared again. Happiness is something to lose.

. . . .

That night we had an agreeable dinner at the guest hall and learned more about our hosts. The woman, Hillim, was studying to be an agricultural planner and spent most of her time reading books on the subject. I could scarcely understand a word of it, since I have approximately zero experience in the subject and following technical conversations in a foreign language is never easy. From what little I gleaned, she was talking about creating gardens that worked like forests, where human involvement could be kept to a minimum. She was a fascinating conversationalist, however, and once you were used to it, her speech impediment wasn't really a problem.

Sjolis, however, the man, was deaf, and the sign language in Hron had seemingly nothing—not even grammar, somehow—in common with the sign language I knew. When he joined the conversation, he did so by first signing to Hillim, who relayed his words to us. He helped in the fields, he said, and he liked to climb, but he didn't know what he wanted to do with his life. He'd thought about joining a Free Company, but he also wasn't sure he wanted to spend time away from Hillim.

Hillim and I had made sweetcakes for dessert and we served them to our friends with smiles on our faces. No one was drunk, but everyone was merry. We played parlor games like Secrets Of The Stone and Faced With Eternity into the small hours of the morning, telling one another our stories and fears and hopes.

But much to my displeasure, we decided we could stay only one night in Holl. Winter would only set in worse, and there was no way Grem or I would be skiing anytime soon. If we wanted to reach Hronople, we had to beat the snow.

When I signed the guest log in the morning, in addition to going on at length about the brilliance of the facilitator I'd witnessed, I wrote:

"Holl is my favorite town in all of Hron so far. I spent an entire day here and not a single person tried to murder me."

Thirteen

The river Keleni runs southwest out from the spine of the Cerracs, fed by snowmelt from the caps of Mt. Nisit and Mt. Raum. It runs through the Keleni valley, what many might call the heart of the Cerracs, and then, at the southern edge of the plateau, it drops off the edge. Keleni Falls is one of the largest waterfalls in the world, I was told, two hundred yards wide and dropping almost half a mile into the canyon below.

Hronople is built spanning the river and the top of the falls, so as soon as we crossed through into the valley, we saw rainbows in the mist emerging from the city walls. The entire place is roughly medieval in appearance—odd considering the bulk of the city is no greater than thirty years old—though the architectural biases of the Cerracs were present as well in the stone-and-glass designs with fiercely sloped roofs. Hronople is a work in progress, but the largest buildings are in the north, the furthest from the falls, and they descend in height down from there, giving the entire thing the look of a grand staircase. This design was implemented to catch the best of the winter sun, I was told.

Here the hack *Review* writer in me comes out, because I'm

tempted to speak in superlatives, the likes of which I ascribed to cities I'd never seen when I used to write articles for the travel section. Yes, the city was charming, quaint, unique—a "must-see" even. But I cannot divorce the sight of the city from the experience of my journey to reach it, and more than anything when I saw Hronople I saw hope. Even with the city walls only half-built, the place looked formidable. The pass we'd ridden through couldn't support an army at march with machines of war and the home-terrain advantage would be nigh unsurmountable. The war felt far behind me.

The closer we got to the city, the more Sorros relaxed and became more the man I'd first known at the front—when the road took us through a young forest populated by oak and nut trees, he took delight in pointing out the edible plants growing everywhere. It was as much a garden as a forest, he explained, much like our host in Holl had described.

The sun, low on the southern horizon, cast a faint glow on us through the haze. It was occasionally warm on my face, but mostly I was surrounded by the bitter cold of a mountain midwinter. Yet as we approached closer to the city, we rode past people in their shirtsleeves at work inside enormous greenhouses built of plate glass and wrought iron.

"How's that work?" I asked, pointing towards one such group of gardeners.

"There're thermal vents under the whole valley," Sorros explained. "This was the winter home for half the towns in the Cerracs five hundred years back, and the Hronople engineers are masters of harnessing the heat of the earth." It was clear from the way he gestured and spoke that he took no small amount of pride in the ingenuity of his people.

"What happened, then?" I asked.

"Pardon?"

"This place *was* the winter home. Why happened?"

"Oh, the Rift. One town decided it owned the place and wanted to move here permanently. The other ones weren't so keen on that, and, well, words turn to knives sometimes, you know? When it was over, everyone decided to leave the place alone. Too many ghosts, whether literal or metaphorical, for most people's liking."

"Hronople is the city of ghosts," Nola said. "Hron means 'ghost' in Old Vorronian."

"When the refugees poured in, there must have been fifty thousand of them, there was nowhere else for them to go," Sorros said. "My mom, my birth mom, used to tell me what a nightmare the whole thing was. The villages didn't have much to do with one another back then, not on any organizational level, and while there was some resentment for the foreigners getting one of the nicest valleys around, there wasn't any real desire to stop them either."

"Wait," I said, "hold on. 'Hron' means 'ghost?' Your country is named 'ghost?'"

Nola nodded, but Sorros answered. "When it started, I think the idea was that the whole concept of having a name, of needing to name your country, really only mattered in the context of comparing ourselves with other societies. And what are ghosts? Ghosts are invisible and you can't hurt them, but they haunt you by the memory of their presence. The refugees really liked that angle, the idea of being an invisible country that still affects those around it. I think the rest of us went for it because we mostly didn't care and didn't really see ourselves in conversation with people from outside of Hron anyway."

"But that's not how it turned out," I said. "The other night we toasted to Hron. There's a patriotism here, at least in the younger generation."

"True," Sorros said.

"Does that matter?"

"No idea," Sorros said. "Maybe."

"Do you have a flag?" I asked.

"No."

"Should you?" I asked.

"Why would we want a flag?"

"Symbols mean something. Like ghosts. They're not real but they affect everything."

"Okay," Sorros said, "I'm curious. What does Borolia get from having a flag?"

I thought about it for awhile. It was nice to have something to think about other than how much I was tired of riding. "It's easier when you're an empire to want a flag," I admitted. "Borolia wants to see the gold-and-green hanging over more and more houses, over more and more cities. In the war room at the *Review*, we had a big map on the wall and we moved little flags around the board as the front shifted."

"We don't need that," Sorros said. "We have no interest in expansion and honestly we have no interest in imaginary lines anyway."

"What if you lose territory? What if Holl is occupied by Imperial troops?"

"Unless they kill every one of us, they won't have 'occupied' the territory," Sorros said.

"You're evading the question," I said.

"What question is that? What little icon some imperialist

newspaper can put on the war room map to indicate Hron? If we had a flag it would be a black one. The negation of a flag."

"Or one with a cute little ghost on it," Dory said. I hadn't realized she was listening. "Like what a kid would draw. That's what I'd pick."

"What else do we need a flag for?" Sorros asked.

"When you go off to war," I said, "everything I've read leads me to believe that banners and flags, as symbols, improve morale. It's the tangible object that represents the intangible ideal."

"That's an easy one," Nola said. "I've thought about this a lot. I used to lead troops, and flags inspire loyalty. But in the Free Company we aren't looking for loyalty, we're looking for solidarity, for bravery. For us, it's the mask. We inherited it from the revolutionaries—they used masks when they went into battle so the authorities wouldn't know whom to arrest later. But we keep it up because the mask is something more than that. It's the flag and the uniform all in one—at its simplest, in the middle of a fight I know who my friends are. I know whom to shoot. But more than that I know my friends and myself are one thing, that my own life is only a portion of the whole. I feel powerful with a mask on, as powerful as I ever felt with soldiers at my command who were loyal to the white-and-red."

The conversation took us through the field of greenhouses and out along the Keleni. I caught a strong whiff of sulphur, and soon we passed a group of ten middle-aged women and men relaxing nude in a hot spring, passing around a cigarette. They saw me staring and a few of them waved. I waved back. I wanted to join them.

In front of us loomed the northernmost buildings of the city, built of stone in the late medieval style with delicate flying buttresses and elaborate arched rooftops. Some were bare stone and marble, others had brightly painted reliefs carved into them with varying degrees of skill.

When we reached the unfinished border wall, we passed through what would likely one day become a massive gatehouse, but was at present a literal hole in the wall. On the other side, a dozen youths aged five to fifteen were playing a game that involved shouting prime numbers and tackling one another.

"Afternoon!" a ten-year-old girl called from where she lay underneath a pile of younger children. She shook them off and approached. "Just getting to town?"

"We are," Nola said, dismounting to stand closer to the girl's own height. "What's news?"

"There's a council of war that got called," the girl answered, "but it's not for a few weeks. And the tomato crop failed, and Jol and Simol jumped off the falls and their friends are pretty upset, so if you go to the Cold Quarter expect a cold reception!"

"You've been saving that pun for hours," Nola said, "haven't you?"

"I have."

"Any good news?"

"The winter greens are coming great, my mom says, and Myilin said this morning that both sides of this stupid engineering fight over railroads versus zeppelins have agreed that the fight is stupid so they're starting to talk to each other again. And my dad's back from the mountain for a few days and he brought me a grasshopper the size of my arm. Well not really the size of my arm but it's really big."

"Where can we stable?" Nola asked.

"Myilin said that only Falling Horse Stables is full."

"Thank you," Nola said. "You're doing a great job. Have you been doing welcome gate long?"

"Oh just since lunch," the girl said. "But I did it last month too and last year Bijji used to do it a lot and her and I used to be best friends so I came and played with her a lot while she was doing welcome gate."

We waved farewell to the welcome committee and rode into the city.

"Kids work here?"

"You're doing it again," Sorros said.

"Doing what?" I asked.

"You're judging our country based on your own assumptions. Where you're from, child labor is a bad thing, right?"

"It is," I said. "I hated it."

"The idea is what?" Sorros asked. "That it's bad to force children to do labor because labor is horrible and dangerous and so kids should at least have a chance to grow up some before they are forced into a system of wage slavery?"

"That's... that's not how I would have put it," I said, "but yeah, maybe." I thought about it more. "No, that's not right at all, actually. It's bad for kids to work because they don't have the social capital that adults have, and it's easier to force them into worse work conditions."

"The same argument could be used against making poor people work," Grem suggested.

"People work in Hron because it's fulfilling to do something socially productive and because it's necessary," Sorros said. "We don't force kids to work any more than we force them to eat, to learn, or to play. You know what my favorite game was when I was growing up? My friends and I called it knife-killer. We found out

145

what bugs were bad for the garden and we hunted them down in teams. At the end of the day all the teams piled up the corpses of the bugs they'd killed, and the older kids picked out the ones that were 'valid kills,' the pests, and we counted them all. We were competing against ourselves, against our teams' best previous scores and the best previous scores of the whole lot of us playing. Somewhere in Moliknari, I bet there's still a wooden board we carved the highest collective score from each year. No one called it 'work.'"

"Why'd you skip out on work all the time then?" Dory asked.

Nola started laughing. Even Sorros looked amused.

"Mol told you about that, did he?"

Dory smiled.

We stabled our horses at Nine Swallows Stables, at the edge of town. The stablehands there treated us like royalty—or at least heroes—when Grem explained we were part of a Free Company. The rest of the way we went on foot. This time, at last, Sammit and Dammit came with us.

"Are we staying with you two?" Grem asked.

"We don't have a house," Nola said. "We ran off to play hero."

"Where then?" I asked. "Are there guest halls here?"

"Kind of," Nola said. "But to be honest they're not as nice. Space is at a premium in the city, and so the guest halls are kind of crowded and tend to attract people who..."

"Are terrible at everything?" Sorros suggested.

"I was going to go with 'aren't habitually clean,'" Nola said.

"I like 'are terrible at everything,'" Sorros said. "Though I suppose it's kind of rude."

"Didn't you all..." Grem started.

"Yes, yes," Sorros said, "we met in the Stained Mare, where we were both living. But let's move on from that subject..."

"Where are we staying then?" I asked.

"Friends of my mother's," Sorros said. "Friends of Ekarna."

The city was laid out, like so many cities, in a confusing mixture of a rational grid and a complex and chaotic maze. The closer we got to the heart of the city, the more convoluted and winding the roads and the more impromptu the architecture became. Most of the streets were covered with wood or glass for the winter, and it wasn't long before I had my overcoat over one shoulder and was wishing I was wearing slightly less wool.

More than half the streets seemed more like alleys, and I lost count of the number of bridges I crossed over frozen creeks or the Keleni.

I was counting on the roar of the waterfall to orient me south, but the location of the sound was obscured by the complex streets and soon I was thoroughly lost. But eventually, we came to a three-story stone house with the relief of a two-horned horse carved into the lintel.

Nola smiled, took off her gloves, and opened the door.

....

The two weeks I spent in Hronople were likely the happiest of my life. We stayed in a house overlooking the falls, one of the oldest houses in the city. Eight people lived communally there, sharing a kitchen but each with their own bedrooms. Our hosts were mostly doctors, but for a gardener and a woman named Carhi. When I asked Carhi what she did she told me she was a "layabout" and chastised me for labeling people based on their work preferences. Later, Sorros told me she spent her time studying philosophy and pitching in with odd jobs.

The attic was a fine art workshop space that went largely

unused, and we set our bedrolls down between the easels and bay windows. Each night I spent at that house I went to sleep cuddling Dammit, lulled by the sound of rushing water, and each morning I woke with the winter sun on my face and to the smell of breakfast. Dory and Nola and Sorros went off every day to do soldierly things and Grem spent his time in physical therapy, learning to walk with a prosthetic. I was invited to join the former group, but by and large I declined and spent my time wandering alone.

Hronople is split loosely into various "quarters," each dominated by a different style of living, though each of the quarters bleeds into others. And apparently, the Windrun Quarter and the Iron Quarter actually share an interwoven geography. Which is to say, they are the same place with two different names used by two slightly different cultures of people. Decentralization is a key principle in Hronish decision making (I'd say "governance" but they'd hate me for it), and this rough sectioning off of the city plays an important role in that.

When Sorros explained the system to me, I was expecting something like the nascent gang culture of Borol, where names and identities are important and the lines between gangs are, while fluid, absolutely present. To my surprise and pleasure, this wasn't the case at all. Microcultures formed around all kinds of identities, from work preferences to music preferences to sexual preferences, but I never met anyone (well, anyone over the age of twenty or so) who belonged to only a single group or really came across as committed to the distinction between groups.

I found the Ink Quarter on my third day, with its binderies and libraries and bookshops (the difference between the latter two being rather blurred by the economics of the place) and I'm afraid I let the rest of the city languish a bit after that. I spent most of my time reading, some of my time writing down my notes, and perhaps an embarrassingly small percent of my time helping out at the establishments I was frequenting.

I slept with an older man, in his late thirties, who stewarded one of the stores, and he made me swear up and down that any details about our encounters beyond that would remain between us. "I read books to get away from my life," he said, "and I don't like the idea of ever running across myself while doing so."

The city culture was as warm as the rural culture was cold, and strangers were almost unnervingly open and kind. I made friends quickly and easily—but, I suspected, perhaps not as deeply.

I started acting the journalist again instead of just the wounded soldier, and talked to dozens of people about their lives. On the whole, people seemed happier in Hronople than Borol, but not staggeringly so. They worried about their relationships and their health, they worried about the war, they worried about mortality and the afterlife. They worried about everything I'd grown up worrying about, except work, bosses, and poverty.

While the culture was different in the city than it was in the countryside, the politics were basically the same. I asked numerous people about that, and began to piece together more of Hronish history. When the Vorronian refugees had poured in, they'd brought their anarchist and republican politics with them—two politics with very little overlap. It was the indigenous anarchism that turned the tide against formal government, in the end. The towns and villages simply wouldn't accept any authoritarian governing state—they'd lived without law or money for a thousand years, and just because they were willing to confederate didn't mean they were willing to drop the rest of their beliefs. In the end, any trace of republicanism was wiped out, and the accord was a synthesis of the local methods and those espoused by the refugees.

I still wasn't able to find anyone willing to admit they knew the damn accord by heart, however.

....

A week before the council, Dory tracked me down at the library, dredging me out of my reverie.

"We're going to meet tonight after dinner," she said.

"When's dinner?" I asked. I'd been taking my meals at cafes in the Ink Quarter mostly, and had been to the house only to sleep on the nights I slept alone.

"Now," she said.

I looked at my book. It was marked with a blue X on the inside cover, suggesting that it wasn't for loan. I sighed and put it down, then followed Dory out of the building.

"What were you reading?" she asked.

"It was called *A Page of Heresy*," I told her.

"Vorronian, right?" she asked. "One of the revolutionary texts?"

"Have you read it?" I asked.

"No," she told me. "My parents were into it. It was one of my dad's favorite books. My dad was a refugee—his folks were killed in the First Gasp. My mom said she only liked it because it let her understand my dad better. I tried to read it once, when I was younger, but all that stuff about negativity and nihilism... it probably made sense in Vorronia, but I'm not really sure it does here. Here, I think what matters is how to defend yourself and your friends."

"The introduction of this version mentioned that," I said. "It was the first Cer edition and it talked about how the tactics the main text discusses, such as assassination, workplace sabotage, and the... what did they call it, the 'vandalism of the instruments of banality,' that those were more likely justifiable in the context of... actually, it used some words I didn't really know. My Cer is kind of limited, but basically it seems like those tactics make sense when you're surrounded by government but they don't when you're surrounded by freedom."

Dory nodded. "My favorite books are a bit more practical. My brother goes in for fantasy novels, and I like those too, but I'll take a book on tactics any day. Most philosophy I see seems like it was written to justify whatever the philosopher wanted to do anyway. Why do we need to justify acting on our desires? We should just act on them. The people who think what we're doing is good will tell us, the people who think what we're doing is bad will tell us, and we can use that to inform our future actions."

"That's philosophy," I said.

"You're trying to tease me, I think," Dory said, "not just be rude. Right?"

"Yeah."

"It's not working," she told me. "But I think I'm finally starting to understand you."

"Alright," I said.

We walked through the heated streets of the city, and I watched as people flitted past me, some smiling, some not.

"I miss adventure hour," Dory said.

"Me too," I responded.

"I miss my friends," she said. "The dead ones and the living ones."

We weren't headed to the house, it turned out. I pulled my greatcoat tighter as we left the heated city and strode out to a large, low warehouse just outside the eastern walls. Inside, it was a work-shop, full of furnaces and chains and all the ephemera of industrial production. I saw my travel companions from the Free Company spread out across the small living area along with three strangers. Despite everyone reclining deep into their couches and the spread of food and alcohol on the table, everything seemed tense.

"We're fucked," Sorros said.

"We're not fucked," the first stranger said. She was a woman of about thirty years, with curly red hair and the arms of a smith.

"Well, we might be fucked," the second stranger said. He was young, probably my age, with a distinctive wine-red birthmark running across a large part of his face.

The third stranger, an elderly pale man, said nothing, only scowled from within his deep black hood.

"Dimos," Sorros said as I walked in. "Would you be so kind as to explain to these fine people that we're fucked?"

"Well, I, uh..." I began, stalling. I regained my composure after a moment. "Hi, my name is Dimos."

"Kata," the woman said. "And my husband here is Habik, and the man under the hood goes by the name of Jackal." This last was the Boroli word for the animal.

"They make bombs," Sorros said. "And poison."

"Among other things," Kata said, then turned her attention back to me. "I've heard you're the pre-eminent expert on Borolian military technology. So, well, we'd like very much to know what you know."

"I've never served in His Majesty's Army," I told them, "but I reported on the war for a number of years."

"That's fine," Kata said. "That'll have to do. Vehicles?"

"Borolia's main strength is found in His Majesty's navy," I said.

"That's a mark under the 'we're not fucked' column," Habik said. He picked up a clipboard and made a note.

"They've got hot air balloons," I said.

"Do they carry ordinance?" Kata asked.

"I don't think so," I said. "They don't have the lift. They're used for reconnaissance. And they've got armored carriages, horse drawn, with machine guns up top."

"What's a machine gun?" Habik asked.

"It's a gun that fires four hundred rounds per minute," I answered.

"So... that's a mark under the 'we're fucked' column," Habik said.

"It takes a carriage to carry?" Kata asked.

"A carriage or a train or a ship," I said.

"So the roads, the roads are what matter. We can get by on skis and horses with what we need, and we know the terrain."

"You're going to destroy your own roads?" I asked.

"If it comes to that," Kata said. "We could mine them in places, at the very least, or blow the bridges."

"With what?" Habik asked. "Shotgun shells?"

"What do you mean?" I asked.

Sorros stood up and poured beer into a glass. "We've kind of got a... problem when it comes to military production," he said, handing me the beer.

"We don't do any," Habik said.

"Oh. That could be a problem." I sat down and took a sip. "Why not?"

"It's in the accord," Kata said. "Section six, technology. 'Technologies that are a detriment to the ecosystem reduce the ability for an abundance of life to flourish and thus tend towards the creation of homogenous and unhealthy spaces that deny the relationship of freedom between people.'"

"So you don't do military production because it's bad for the earth?" I asked.

"Basically," Kata said.

"Then who cares about the accord?" Grem said. "I get why we shouldn't start, I don't know, pouring coal into the river on some massive scale, but when it comes down to it why would you let some words on paper keep you from making what we need to survive?"

"A lot of people care about the accord," Kata said. "Especially in Hronople. We need it here more than elsewhere, there are too many of us. I even agree with it: I care about technology, about developing our own production of what we need, but if Hronople turns into a factory town, if we industrialize, we'd lose our soul in the process."

"So what do you three do?" I asked.

"Oh, we make weapons and bombs and armor and poison and all the ephemera of war and battle," Kata said, "but we hold ourselves to strict guidelines in production. There are some iron mines in the hills, but they don't produce prodigious quantities. There are gunsmiths in Hronople, but no more than ten of them, and they craft guns by hand. And coal... we don't do coal."

"What we were talking about before you showed up," Nola said, "is what these three can do, and what the Free Company can do to help them. That's what led us to the conclusion that, as Sorros said so clearly, 'we're fucked.' But while that's a serious possibility, it's not one that does us much good to entertain. So... what do we do?"

"We ask people to pitch in to the war effort," Sorros said. "We get everyone out there mining and smelting and turning rocks into rifles as fast as we can. We start canning food and smoking meats and we turn every scrap of wool into clothes that will get us through the cold spring nights."

"We can do that," Kata said. "And I guess we will. But that's not the three of us. We're research and development. And a lot of our development has been on hold after we lost Bahrit."

"Bahrit?" I asked.

"Bahrit worked here," Sorros said. "Until he decided he didn't care about Hron."

"That... that might be fair," Kata said. "Bahrit was a brilliant man, but he didn't want to hold himself responsible for how he applied that brilliance."

"And?" I asked.

"He's in Karak," Kata said.

"We need him," Habik said.

"The fuck we do," Sorros said.

"We need him," Habik repeated.

"Why has your development been on hold, then?" I asked, eager to change the subject at least a little.

"After one of our coworkers went antisocial," Kata said, "we decided to be even more cautious in our experimentation. Our reputation wasn't looking so good."

"So your obsession with the environment and making sure your neighbors think you're nice people means that your country's research facility doesn't do any military research because it might look bad?" I asked.

"Bahrit released a biological agent into the water supply of the Cold Quarter that killed fourteen people and left more than two hundred with permanent psychological damage," Kata said. "They have nightmares in the day. Every day."

"Oh," I said.

"He took off as soon as it happened," Kata continued. "If I thought he'd done it on purpose I'd track him down and kill him myself... not as revenge, you understand, but because a man who does something like that on purpose is a danger to every living thing in this world. He didn't do it on purpose. He was careless, even reckless, and there's no place for him here."

"We need him," Habik said.

"It won't happen," Kata said, and that was the end of the argument.

The rest of the evening we discussed plans for stealing arms from the enemy, a plan Nola was excited to bring to the rest of the Free Company after the council, though as the night got later we were further and further into our cups. I believe that by the end I had volunteered to assassinate the King himself. Fortunately, such agreements weren't binding.

....

The day before the council, I went back to Nineswallow Stables so that I might go for a ride and see the valley—and return to the hot springs I'd passed on my way into the city. I saw a familiar face tending to the horses.

"Vin?" I asked. It was the farrier who'd run off from His Majesty's Army.

"Dimos!" he shouted, then ran to me, dropping his hammer and catching me in a hug. He kissed me on the mouth in greeting.

"How the hell are you alive?" he asked, and I told him my story, at least the pertinent details.

"And yourself?" I asked.

"My friends who ran, they told me the way out was to run to the villages, to throw yourself at their mercy. It sounded insane, but so did staying." He spat. "I didn't have the courage. But go ahead, ask me how I found the strength to run, to forget the gibbet."

"How?" I asked.

"Alcohol!" he said. "My father taught me the trick. You focus on the thing you want with all your heart, the thing you're too afraid to do, and then you sit down with a flask and focus on what you hope to accomplish. There at the bottom of the bottle you'll find the courage, he said, and he was right."

"Did it ever work for him?" I asked.

"Well he shot his boss," Vin said, "so in a way, yes. Got caught and hanged pretty quick afterwards, so in a way, no."

"But here you are," I said.

A flask appeared in Vin's hand. "A toast to the two of us, who've outlived the maggots of men who wanted us to die."

I drank to that, and he joined me on my ride in the country, and then the next day my bliss came to an immediate and frightening halt.

Fourteen

The council chamber was an amphitheater housed in a drafty old wooden building, nothing like the grand structures I'd seen thus far in the city. But it was, apparently, one of the oldest buildings in Hronople and since it spent most of its time as a venue for performances and theatre, no one had ever gone through the effort of closing it for renovations.

The amphitheater did its job well. The rows of seating were carved from sound-absorbing limestone and the acoustic paneling suspended from the rafters helped keep the acoustics as clear as they could be. Amazingly, despite upwards of two thousand people sitting in on the meetings, most voices could be heard.

The front benches were reserved for the spokespersons from every group that chose to be present. Dory was representing the Free Company, so the rest of us took seats in the back.

There were two people facilitating the proceedings, a white-haired woman who leaned on a cane and spoke with a commanding voice and a younger person whose gender I couldn't distinguish who seemed mostly present to whisper information to the woman.

"We're here for a council of war," the woman said, beginning the meeting. "The first one we've ever had. We've got a process we're going to try, and during the lunch recess and then later tonight after dinner anyone who would like to discuss process may join us and do so. But we have a *lot* to discuss and a lot of people from all over the country who clearly have important things to get done, so we won't be discussing non-immediate process concerns during the meeting itself.

"Before we get started, I just want to clarify for those who haven't been to confederational councils before that this is not a decision-making body. This is a coordinating body. The decision making will happen in the groups that you each represent. We'll hear from a few witnesses and experts about the threat that we face, then we'll hear from each spokesperson about their plans. Concerns about plans may be raised but we are not here to police one another's actions, only to give ourselves the knowledge we need to integrate our plans with one another so as to defend ourselves from this threat. Spokespersons will take the information they have learned today back to their groups and develop their plans, and we will have monthly confederational councils to discuss developments until that is no longer practical."

"Does that really work?" I whispered to Nola. "You were an officer... can you really organize a war without a central decision maker?"

"I don't know," she admitted. "We've never had to try it before. In theory, though, it's got a lot going for it. It encourages initiative... hierarchy is notoriously slow. The worst of both worlds would be a committee though, some kind of central decision-making body that has to come to agreement with everyone. I'm glad we didn't end up going for that."

I was called down to the stage to present the case I'd made so many times before, giving my estimation of troop strength and likely timing, then Nola was called to discuss the command structure of the army she'd spent years fighting against. Others discussed road conditions and geography. Vin talked about conscription and horses.

Then Dory, for the Free Company, stood up and told them our plan to patrol the mountain passes and kill any soldiers they saw. It sounded simple and elegant the way she put it and her words were interrupted by applause near the end of every sentence until the facilitator asked for people to keep their cheering until the end of her speech. After going over our rather simplistic plan, Dory stated what we might have to offer other groups—information about troop movements and resources scavenged from the corpses we would make—and what we might be looking for from other groups: recruits, munitions, safe houses, and supplies.

One by one, spokespersons from all over the country took their turn to discuss their plans. Some details like exact locations were intentionally left out, I discovered, owing to the risk of spies. The crowd seemed about half groups committed to support—miners and farmers and engineers—and half groups committed to fighting.

After lunch, Vin took another turn in front of the audience. "I represent a group that doesn't have a name yet, about forty strong. My friends and I are from Tar," he said. "We're new to your country and we love it and what it stands for in the way only immigrants can. We were trained to fight in His Majesty's Army as conscripts, but we escaped. Our plan is to return to Tar and, if need be, destroy it."

His words were met with wild cheers.

"You've already given us so much. So all I'm asking for now are your trust and your advice about what we can do in Vorronia."

A few people from the audience stood and formed a line in the aisle, then addressed Vin's question one at a time, speaking loudly to the audience.

"Kill their commanders," the first man suggested while he gently rocked a baby in a sling across his chest.

"Sabotage their military factories and the rail lines that bring troops to the front," a young woman—a girl, really, likely no more than thirteen—added.

"Foment revolt," the next person said.

Kata stood next, the last person in line. "Steal engineering plans," she suggested.

"The hell with Tar! Get to Borol! Kill the king!" someone shouted from the audience. The younger facilitator stared them down for speaking out of turn.

"Thank you," Vin said. "We'll consider your advice."

The next person to stand up was an elderly man, discussing what role the leatherworker's syndicate of Hronople might offer the war effort, but he hadn't gotten far when Joslek, from the Free Company, bounded into the chambers and down the steps, panting to catch his breath before whispering to the facilitators.

The young facilitator then whispered to the leatherworker, who nodded and stood aside. Joslek stepped forward.

"They're here," he said, not quite loudly enough. The chamber went silent. "Three days ago. Ten thousand troops. They've taken Moliknari. Wiped out..." he stopped talking, leaned forward to take deep breaths and master his emotions. "They've wiped out the Free Companies of the Falls, Birch Root, Owl Skull, Laughter, and Mountain Heather."

The room erupted. Dory ran to Joslek and embraced him. Sorros was crying, and Nola put an arm around him.

"How do we respond?" the older facilitator asked.

Grem stood up and hobbled down the steps on his prosthetic with the help of a cane. He stood facing the crowd until it quieted some to hear him out.

"We kill them," he said. "We kill them all."

Fifteen

"This is good news for us," Nola said, back at the house. The living room was in terrible disrepair, filled with the possessions of at least a dozen people preparing to leave for the front at first light.

"Ten thousand soldiers invade while we're catching our breath, that's a good thing? My mother's death, the destruction of my home..." Sorros drifted off, too numb to sustain his anger.

Nola clasped his hand in hers. "Winter in the Cerracs is deadly enough for those of us who know the mountains," she said. "They caught us unprepared, it's true, and they hit us hard. But one of us on skis is worth a dozen of them on foot. The conditions simply couldn't be better for guerilla war."

"Fuck your conditions for warfare," Sorros said.

"You going to give up?" Nola asked.

Sorros let go of her hand and stormed off.

The three weapons researchers came in. Habik was calm, almost frighteningly so, but Kata's eyes were red from tears and she could scarcely look anyone in the eye. Jackal was unreadable, as always.

"What's news?" Nola asked.

"There are three thousand willing to leave tomorrow," Habik

said. "Youth who've been training with the militia for years, and youth just old enough to tell their parents they're going regardless. Women and men in their twenties who've never handled a gun in their life have volunteered by the hundreds. They'll train at night along the way, and any of them who survive will train harder later. And finally, more than a thousand women and men who call themselves the gray brigade—veterans of the revolution, not a woman of them under fifty."

Nola nodded.

"There's something I'd ask of you," Kata said, softly. "Or of anyone, really."

"Anything we can do to help the you three help us win this war," Nola said.

"Get Bahrit," Kata said. "Get Karak. If the gray brigade and these kids are able to push back the first wave, so what? Borolia outnumbers us five to one and it's been a military state for longer than we've had an accord. Bahrit won't talk to us, I'm sure of it, but he might talk to you. Convince him to lend his strength to ours."

"How?" Nola asked.

"Amnesty?" Habik suggested.

"It'll never work," Sorros said, returning to the room. "People in Karak don't want amnesty, they want to live in their own way. Their own shitty, backstabbing, antisocial way."

"Then please," Habik said. "Think of something. There are eight thousand people there and to be frank, they know how to fight. And who knows what Bahrit has been designing, without the accord?"

"If we let them in as an army, what's to keep them from staying?" Sorros said. "No, I won't have it."

"You of all people," Habik said. "I thought you'd understand."

I've never seen Sorros so angry. To his credit, he mastered it better than anyone I've ever seen. His face and his fists tightened and relaxed rhythmically and he only spoke after five, maybe six breaths. "I, of all people, understand what it means to commit yourself to betterment. I, of all people, know what the mind of a man who has chosen to betray his fellows is thinking. I, *of all people*, will not have it."

Nola interceded. "I've recruited Sorros for a plan of my own," she said. "We're going to the front, and if we survive, we're headed into Vorronia with the ex-conscripts. We'll strike at the prisons, free the people inside. Those people have been condemned to die in cells, have never had the chance to be accepted by a free society. We'll offer those people that chance, not Karak."

"I'll go," I said.

"What?" Sorros asked.

"I'll go to Karak. Tomorrow. I'm damn near useless in a gun-fight and to be honest I hope I'm never in another one. But what Habik says sounds true."

"You can't," Sorros said.

"Can't?" I asked. "Am I not free?"

"You're free, journalist. I've never put you in ropes, not once. But you can't simply offer amnesty to those who live outside the society that we've made. You're free to offer them only your personal amnesty, and I suspect that once you meet them you won't want to."

"I won't negotiate with them," I said. "I get it. I've got nothing to offer them. But I *will* tell them about the ten thousand foreigners who are marching through the mountains burning and killing, and we'll see what they do."

"We will indeed," Sorros said.

"I will join you," Jackal said, startling me and everyone else in the room. His voice was a baritone and it seemed to shake the bone. I looked at him for clarification, but he said nothing else.

"Jackal wasn't working with us yet when Bahrit left," Kata said. "So Bahrit might not having anything against him.

"Well pack your shit too, then," Sorros said. "I guess we're all leaving tomorrow. If you get any of those bastards to fight, meet us in Holl. That'll likely be our headquarters."

....

Most of Hronople came out to see the Gray Brigade off. The old veterans didn't march, per se, but walked with their masked faces high. Some held hands, some walked in lines with their arms linked together. Others stood alone. One in three of them had a firearm, the others bore spears, swords, or improvised explosives. Some walked with war dogs—or dogs who had become war dogs—and some did not.

My friends had ridden out in the frozen gloaming, as much to avoid the spotlight as to make certain no one commandeered their mounts, and they brought two hundred trained warriors with them. At least once a day, every day until I saw them next, I had to fight panic as I worried about them.

The war was to our north and west, but I left that day with Jackal to ride to the southeast on two mountain ponies. We rode hard the entire day on unfamiliar forest roads, just at the edge of our ponies' endurance, and camped for the night in the ruins of a long-abandoned, roofless stone church.

"You don't talk much," I said as I lit a fire with scraps of lumber from the ruin.

"I do not speak Cer," the man said.

"Do you speak Boroli?" I asked, in Boroli.

He looked at me without comprehension. "I do not speak Cer," he said again in Cer. "My name is Jackal. I am of Dededeon."

"I don't speak Deded," I said, in Deded. I could say maybe ten words in ten tongues.

He nodded.

I roasted some hare, which he refused, but ate nuts and dried fruit from his bag, then made enough tea for the two of us. It was herbal, with clove and nutmeg and something else I couldn't identify, but it did wonders for casting the chill from my skin.

After dinner, he pulled a tin whistle from his bag and played a tune, a sparse tune in a style that was completely foreign to me, but one I could appreciate the beauty of. Then he put it down and sang, and he did so with more strength and more passion than anyone I'd ever heard. His songs were long and winding, moving from staccato words to opera to an almost jolly rhythm. I fell asleep to his foreign words.

....

The next day I implored him to teach me Deded as we rode. I've got a good head for languages, though of course without the aid of writing or a shared tongue, I mostly learned verbs and nouns. Still, it gave us something to focus on other than the seemingly imminent death of our friends, our adopted country, and likely ourselves.

The third day, we found ourselves in canyons and Jackal led the way confidently through a maze carved by rivers and rain. The cold weather kept the risk of flash flooding at bay, though it meant fording even a stream was a life-or-death activity.

What I knew from the map I'd seen in Hronople was that Karak was at the southeastern edge of Hron, tucked in at the border of the country Ora, at least a two day ride from the nearest town large enough to be worth marking down. I knew almost nothing about Ora but what I'd read—and written—in the papers: a savage land at war with itself, the home of the pirates that ply the Blackwater Sea. It was, I had read, a place of class divisions that made Borol look like a utopia: the princes lived in towers built from silver and ivory, the poor lived in shacks built from the ribcages of huge beasts. And both, if stories were to be believed, had acquired the taste for human flesh. Still, they were among the most technologically advanced societies in the world, and Borolian traders ran routes to Ora through the Northern Ocean and down into the Blackwater, risking ice storms and pirates for the chance to trade silver and gold for machinery and plans.

The Oran bandits found us on the fourth night. So far from the front, we hadn't set up a watch, and with the weather so cold we hadn't put out our fire. This is one of the dangers of living in a society so polite as Hron, I realized when I woke with a pistol held to my throat—it was easy to leave your guard down.

There were six of them, all men, their heads shaved and their beards full and long. They wore suit jackets and wool overcoats and no masks—they were clearly not from Hron.

"What do you want?" I asked in Cer.

Most of the men didn't understand my words, but one of them, a teenager with serious acne, did. "We'll take everything," he said. "Your ponies, your guns, your food, your clothes. You'll walk with us for awhile until we decide what to do with you and if you're really good, we might not kill you."

I looked over to Jackal, who couldn't understand our words. His hands were shaking like an alcoholic's and he tried to dodder over to his saddlebags. "Make not-us drink brandy," he said, using pidgin Deded so I could understand.

"Keep away from there!" one of the bandits yelled, bringing the butt of his rifle down on Jackal's arm, knocking him to the ground.

"What did that old man say?" the boy asked.

"Make not-us drink brandy," Jackal repeated.

"He's an alcoholic," I said. "Look at his hands. He's got a bottle of brandy in his saddlebag there, he needs it."

"What?" one of the bandits asked, in Oran.

The boy answered back, speaking far too quickly for me to follow. I can't do much more than introduce myself and curse in Oran.

The man who'd hit Jackal rummaged through the saddlebag, came out with a smokey tinted bottle. He uncorked it, smelled, and took a swig.

"It's good," he said, passing it around. Everyone drank, but they refused to pass it to the boy, laughing at his protestations.

They began to rifle through our things. Then, less than a minute later, every one of them but the boy fell over in pain and died. Jackal reached into his coat, pulled out a chicken's egg, and threw it at the boy's head. It exploded on impact, destroying half the kid's face.

"Egg of god," Jackal said, in Cer.

"Holy fuck," I said, in Deded. Nausea came unbidden to my mind and bile rose in my throat—I swallowed it down.

We robbed their corpses of food and weapons, then, laden down, continued on our way in the moonlight.

Sixteen

I could smell the city before I saw it, the first time I'd had to breathe in the fumes of industry since I'd left Tar. On the fifth afternoon we left the canyons behind and dismounted as we started down a shallow grade on a treacherous road of ice and mud. There wasn't a tree in sight, but where the snow was thinner I saw a forest of stumps. The road bent around the hill, and Karak lay before us.

It was bigger than I'd seen it in my head, covering a decent portion of the valley floor. The town was laid out like a pear, bisected by the single main road. At the northern edge, the top of the pear, along the road, was a shanty town of canvas and wood, but further south it looked like any frontier town in Vorronia, with wood houses of two and three stories and two factory buildings that spit smog into the sky.

Subconsciously, I checked that my pistol was holstered at my side, my brass knuckles in my satchel. Our other weapons were hidden in blankets on our mount.

We walked our ponies into town and eyes peered out from glass windows or wooden, pane-less slats. The first well-built house we walked past was a one-story schoolhouse with a flat roof, cleared of snow and full of playing children. The tension began to release from my body.

Two blocks on, we tied up our mounts on a hitching post outside what looked for all the world like a Borolian public house, with frosted-glass windows and white clapboard walls. We walked into a cloud of smoke—tobacco and opium and stranger herbs—and I was immediately taken back to my days on the street.

Twenty women and men filled the place, lounging on barstools and chairs, one man sitting on a table, precariously perched between full glasses of beer. Half the eyes in the room were on us, and only half of those looked friendly.

"Horacki?" I heard my name, turned, and saw a soldier I'd met while riding with Wilder. The young man who'd been at the Grinder.

I stepped back and put on my brass knuckles. Especially with a wounded arm, I probably should have gone for my gun, but habits are what they are.

"Easy," he said in Boroli. "I'm not looking for a fight."

"You're a soldier," I said.

"Was a soldier," he replied.

We had the room's full attention. Conversations dropped off, and with no music playing, all I heard was the drip of some unseen faucet.

"Can I get a beer for my friends here?" the man cried out. The room went back to its business, but I wasn't about to let down my guard.

A kid—no more than eight—brought us each a tall ceramic mug of beer. I held mine but didn't drink it. Jackal did the same.

"You really don't trust me," he said, "do you?"

"No," I said. "I don't."

He took the mug from me and drank, then licked the foam from his lips.

"Fuck the army," he said. "Fuck His Majesty. You know what? I never had a home and now I do."

I thought he was drinking from the beer to prove it wasn't poisoned, but he didn't give it back.

"And you know what else?" he said. "You think you're better than me because the King didn't give you a rifle. You think you don't have as much blood on your hands as I do. So fuck you too."

He turned his back on me and walked back to a corner to sit with his friends.

I walked up to the bar. The kid was standing on a stool behind it.

"Where can I find Bahrit?"

"Factory," he said.

I probably should have figured that out myself. We left the bar and walked our ponies the rest of our way through town unmolested.

The sun was already low on the horizon, and only one factory had a light on inside, so it was easy to choose which to approach. When we walked up to the double-doors, a middle-aged man in a top hat and a leather coat stepped out of the building.

"Can I help you gentleman?" he asked, in a Vorronian accent.

"We're looking for Bahrit," I replied.

"What's your business with him?"

"I'd prefer to speak to him directly," I answered.

"Why would *he* prefer it that way?"

"Sorry," I said. "I don't mean any offense. We're here with urgent news from Hron and have a lot to discuss with him."

"Well, leave your guns with me, then," the man said. "There are a lot of people from Hron who have more to discuss with Bahrit than he might be willing to talk about. Things like retribution and revenge, or whatever nice terminology they'd come up with for it. Accountability maybe."

I nodded, and handed him my pistol. Jackal looked at me, then followed my lead.

"Your names?" he asked.

"Dimos Horacki," I said. "And this gentleman is Jackal. You?"

"Olevander Bahrit," he answered, "though it seems everyone just calls me Bahrit. Can we go inside? It's cold as shit out here."

Inside the factory was as strange a sight as I'd seen yet in my adventures. In so many ways—the conveyors, the stacked pieces of who knows what machines, the furnace heat—it was like any factory in Borol. But the workers here, the dozen or so I saw, seemed to set their own pace, and as many were staffing the assembly line as relaxed in comfortable chairs, drink in hand, chatting loudly to be heard over the roar of the machinery.

"Much better," Bahrit said, leading us to a small coffee table in one corner of the shop floor where we took seats.

I stripped off my overcoat, set my hat on the table, and wondered if the man might be partly deaf if this was his idea of better. I focus better in the cold, it turns out, than in the tumult of a factory floor.

"What brings you to Karak, Mr. Horacki?"

"Borolia has invaded Hron," I told him. "They've burned Sotoris and captured Moliknari. Ten thousand soldiers are marching, presumably, towards Hronople and they're killing everyone who stands in their way."

Bahrit nodded, pouring himself a thick liquor from a closed-top pitcher on the table. It smelled like solvent.

"I've heard you're the smartest man in Hron," I lied.

"We're not in Hron anymore," Bahrit said. "We're in Karak, no-man's land."

"Hron might fall without your help. Your help specifically, and the help of anyone here trained to fight."

"Are you here to offer us amnesty?" he asked, sipping at his drink.

"No," I said. "I'm one man—I can't offer you a country's amnesty. I suspect people will look with more favor on anyone who comes to fight, but I also..." This was the gamble I'd worked out in my head on the trip. "I suspect that you and most of the people here don't want amnesty at all."

"Oh?" Bahrit asked. "What do you think we want?"

"I can't presume to say."

Bahrit smiled at my words and responded. "I asked for coal once in Hronople, from the miners up north. I know they're bringing it out of the mountain along with everything else, but they wouldn't let me have it. They said 'we can't burn coal, it'll smoke up the air.' I tried to build a factory once, to produce ammunition at faster than artisan speeds. 'You can't build a factory,' the construction syndicate told me. 'Humans aren't meant to be alienated from the products they produce.' So yes, I'm happy in Karak, where I'm free to do as I please."

He gestured towards the workers on the line, who seemed engaged with their labor. "Not everyone wants to be a gunsmith. Yornos there, he's a songwriter. Hli designed the sawmill—I help out there from time to time. Notra... she killed a man on the road and no one in Hron took her side. She's a hunter, but spends the winters helping out in the factories so she has something to do. Karak is no paradise, nor does it pretend to be. We had ten murders in town last year, and before I started sleeping in the factory someone—probably someone I know and trust—broke in here and stole every last bullet we'd poured, probably sold them to Ora. And what I did in Hronople is simply inexcusable. No one should forgive me for that. But you know what? I've had to move on with my life, even though I ended many others."

"So you won't help us?" I asked.

"Oh, I'm going to help you," he answered. "I just wanted you to understand me. I'm going to help you because the bandits from Ora are getting worse and more desperate, and while we've handled them so far, we could use a pact of mutual defense. Us anarchists have to stick together—even if I think they're a bunch of stuck up bastards and they think I'm a murderous fuck. I suspect we'll be able to raise a sizable force."

"Can I have a drink?" I asked.

"I just thought you'd be too good for our swill," Bahrit said, pouring me a tumbler. "One for this gentleman? Who is he, besides a creepy walking corpse? He doesn't understand Cer, am I right."

"He's from Dededeon. Military researcher in Hronople."

"A man after my own heart," Bahrit said, pouring Jackal a glass.

The three of us toasted, and I downed their swill. I had not been deceived by its solvent smell.

....

It took only a day to mobilize the Karak militia for war. Word of the invasion went around that night, and in the morning they had a meeting. It lacked the formality of the councils I'd witnessed in Hron, and little effort was made to make room for lesser-heard voices, but they reached a tentative agreement rather quickly: anyone who wanted to was encouraged to join in the fight against Borolia. They would fight to free Hron, to secure an agreement of mutual defense, and, it was stated quite explicitly, to shove it in Hron's face that it couldn't survive without the men and women of Karak.

Dal, a woman fluent in Deded and Cer, offered to interpret for Jackal and Bahrit, and I spent the day in their company packing ammunition into crates and discussing the machinery of war.

"What happened with those bandits?" I finally had the chance to ask Jackal.

"I've been working with cardiotoxic snake venom for decades," he said, by way of Dal. "I'm immune to it. And, I have to say, I have developed a taste for a brandy only I can drink."

"And the egg?" I asked.

"Gunpowder and a primer," he said. "The primer is kept in a hummingbird egg inside the larger crow's egg. Breaks on impact and explodes. The crow's egg is thickly lacquered with tree sap to keep it from breaking during transport."

Bahrit and Jackal discussed industrial production for awhile, and Bahrit led us from the arms factory to the second factory across the street, filled with body armor.

"Here," Bahrit said, handing me a block of white ceramic about two inches thick, "take a look at this. Look closely at the grain of it."

I held it up to my face, looking for a grain pattern, but none was visible. I heard a gunshot, and the plate cracked in my hands, sending shards of ceramic towards my face. Fortunately, none cut me or got in my eyes. I dropped the plate and saw Bahrit standing with a pistol aimed at my head.

"You're fucking crazy!" I shouted.

"The heat generated by coal power—we get the coal by raiding trains in Ora, no one here wants to mine the stuff apparently, myself included—lets us get kilns so hot that we can turn clay, well not just any clay, into something that'll stop bullets."

I was shaken as badly as I'd been in battle, and I started to walk around to curb the inevitable adrenaline that began to flood my system.

My company seemed unperturbed by the demonstration, and Jackal was incredibly enthusiastic.

"It'll only stop small arms, for now," Bahrit said, "and only the first shot, but it's lighter and stronger than steel. We put these plates into pockets built into vests, or mold the whole thing into helmets."

Soon after, the conversation between the two men fell into small talk, and Dal announced she was going home.

"Are you coming with us?" I asked.

"No," she said.

"Why not?"

"Because I don't feel like it," she responded, then walked out.

....

That night there was a party in the militia hall, the largest interior space in town. The building was drafty and cold, with unfinished walls, and barrels of burning coal and wood provided the only heat. There was plenty of liquor to go around, and for the first several hours, people seemed happy enough. Small bands of musicians took their turns playing for the enthusiastic crowd, playing mostly uptempo jigs and reels with catchy choruses about death and honor and alcohol and sex.

Jackal kept to himself, drinking from a bottle of poison, so I walked through the crowd and tried to make friends.

"You're the guy from Hron, right?" The speaker was a short

woman in a floor-length black dress and gaudy bright makeup around her eyes. She stood in a circle of similarly-clothed androgynous folks.

"I suppose," I answered. It amused me to suddenly be the man from Hron, a country I'd spent such a short period of time in.

"What do you think of Karak?" she asked.

"It's different," I answered.

"Fuck your diplomacy," she said. "What do you think of Karak?"

"I honestly don't know," I said. "I'm from Borol, really, and I don't know what to make of this place at all. What do *you* think of it?"

"It's alright," she said. "It's better than home. I left Hron because I wanted, you know, I wanted real freedom."

She offered me a drink from her wineskin, and the whiskey therein I'm happy to say tasted worlds better than what I'd had with Bahrit.

Behind my new companions, I saw two men exchanging angry words. Soon, they were shoving one another, and the crowd opened up a circle to watch.

The main aggressor, six foot six and built like a bear, threw the first punch and missed. His antagonist, a heavy-set gentleman with gray walrus whiskers, kicked the tall man's knee and soon the two were scrapping on the ground. The crowd cheered.

"Shouldn't we do something?" I asked.

The woman shrugged. "They've got some shit to work out, it looks like."

Karak was a town of street kids, all grown up. It was like watching something I myself had done at fifteen, but these were adults.

The taller man, the one I would have put my money on were

I into such macabre sport, was soon pinned and the walrus man starting bashing his fist into the man's temple. Repeatedly.

"He's going to kill him," I said.

"Might be," the woman said. "Probably not."

Soon, the loser was unconscious—I could see a bubble of blood pop out of his nose, so he was still breathing—and the winner had stumbled off, drunk and wounded, into the crowd.

"What would have happened if he'd killed him?" I asked.

"Probably nothing," the woman replied. "Maybe it would have gotten bad, dragged everyone into it. But probably nothing."

An excited young man came up to join us. "So Roka told Sar that he knew about Sar's brother's defection to Ora," he said, clearly hoping to impress my new friends with this knowledge. "And he said he hoped he'd get to kill Sar's brother himself. So Sar tried to hit him, and, wow, that old man can fight!"

Everyone started laughing. I departed.

....

The sun was past its zenith before the seventeen Freer Companies of Karak—as they styled themselves—left for the north, almost twenty-five hundred strong. Most were on skis, with the ponies largely carrying supplies or dragging sledges. Jackal and I rode our ponies and kept to ourselves. He played music every night, and taught me the words. I'd never spent so long in the company of someone I couldn't speak to, and it frustrated me not to have a grammar book, but I think we became friends regardless.

I was eager to reach Holl, to see my friends, to ascertain they were still alive. His Majesty's troops must have come in fast, arriving less than a month after Wilder's death, and I doubted they had any interest in a long winter campaign.

The two weeks I spent in the company of the Freer Companies taught me almost everything I've come to know and treasure about anarchism, largely by negative example. Freedom, I think, isn't enough. You need freedom and responsibility paired together. As Sorros would say, freedom is a relationship between people, not an absolute and static state for an individual.

Oh, to be sure, the men and women of Karak (and it was largely men, in about a 3-2 ratio with women) were decent people, or at least better people than those I'd met in His Majesty's Army, but I never felt safe in their company. Just like the streets. I'd met some of the most amazing people I've ever known while homeless, but a gutter rat will fight over scraps. When the police and all of polite society has rejected you, the only safety you have is the safety you make, and it's dangerous to ever look weak, to ever put down your guard. It's dangerous to cry. The gutter rat life is a form of anarchy, perhaps, but it wasn't one that ever suited me. Karak seemed much the same.

After fifteen days, we reached the valleys I had known, and our pace slowed as we doubled the scouts. The seventeenth day, at dinner, the scouts reported what they'd seen.

"The Free Companies are holed up in Holl," a young woman said, "They've got barricades up, and trenches, but they're pinned down. Maybe a thousand men blocking them off to the west, slowly working their way around."

"So we'll go in and kill them," a man my own age said, with the arrogance of youth. "And save the day."

That night we drank half the booze we'd brought. And in the morning, when we set off hungover, the end of the trip in sight, ready to be the heroes, we were ambushed.

Seventeen

We broke camp as usual, slowly, lingering over breakfast and carsa, then set out on our skis along the snowed-over and frozen bank of some nameless creek. I was near the fore, as was my habit, and the first gunshots were far off.

The first two reports that I heard, I assumed there was fighting amongst one of the companies. There hadn't been a substantial number of brawls en route, but I figured that for a fluke. But when the shots kept coming, and were met with more gunfire from elsewhere, I knew we were in battle.

"Take cover!" a man yelled.

"Fuck that! Kill the motherfuckers!" another voice called out.

As a force, we'd drawn thin, spread out in a line more than a mile long. The firing was coming from the middle. I dismounted, pulled down my mask, checked my pistol, unslung my rifle and, for better or worse, ran towards the mass of militia that were skiing with all haste towards the tumult.

The first strike had been targeted. No sooner had chaos broken out amongst our ranks than a gatling gun opened fire on us from a placement somewhere close above us in the hills, and the roar of the guns was deafening. The entire mountain was alive with sound and soon blood was melting the snow like piss.

I took cover behind a rock. Jackal was nearby, hiding behind his dead pony.

"Dimos!" he shouted.

"Jackal!" I replied.

"Catch!" he said, and he threw an egg of god at me. Well, more like *to* me, in a light overhand lob, but it was all I could do to reach out and catch the bomb instead of flinching away. I caught it, and it didn't kill me. I set it down and put crampons on my boots, then picked up the bomb. I unholstered my pistol, decided I might need the grip of a free hand, and re-holstered it. I waited for a break in the tat-tat-tat-tat of the gatling gun, then ran. I scrambled up the bank as best I could, then saw the gun placement. The gunner must have seen me, because the gatling gun spun its ten-barrel nose towards me. I dropped to the ground and breathed in, savoring the last air I expected to ever breathe.

I heard an explosion nearby—Jackal must have thrown a bomb himself into the hillside. I stood and scrambled a few more paces while the gunner was distracted, then hurled my egg with what strength I had. It struck the gun and broke through the rock-and-snow gun placement. I charged in, saw two stunned soldiers, and shot them both in the head and took their pistols.

The gatling gun had been destroyed by the egg, and I wouldn't have been able to operate it anyway. Jackal, unable to navigate his way up the icy hill, stayed in hiding, peering out to lob bombs and shoot at the soldiers fool enough to approach.

I thought about waiting out the battle in the gun placement, but decided I would never live with myself if I did. I thought about using my rifle to try to pick out enemy soldiers in the melee below, but realized with my absolute lack of training, I was as likely to hit my own side as the enemy. So instead, I came to terms with my own death once more and ran along the hill, dropping in behind the next gun placement. The gunner was busy spitting death on those below, but his companion saw me coming and shot at me twice. His first shot got me in the chest, knocking me back, but the ceramic vest I wore saved my life. I jumped into the gun placement. With a two-handed grip, I shot the gunner in the chest and turned in time to see a saber slashing down at me. The next thing I knew, I pummeled the man to death with the butt of my gun. And at that, the fighting was over.

Afterwards, I washed my hands in the snow and breathed deep.

....

"Where are we at?" I asked. There were about a hundred of us standing in a semicircle, protected from the weather and stray bullets by a cliff face.

"Two hundred dead. Half a hundred wounded," someone answered.

"And the enemy?" someone asked.

"A hundred dead."

"Any survivors?" I asked.

"Not anymore."

"They ambushed two thousand people with one hundred?" someone asked. "Are they brave or insane?"

"Neither," someone said. It was the ex-soldier, the one I'd accidentally snubbed at the public house in Karak. I still didn't know his name. "They're soldiers. They get orders and they follow them."

"So... insane."

....

We were on the march an hour later. The wounded stayed behind to bury the dead and a crew of doctors and medics stayed to treat them.

By afternoon, we stood at the top of the pass and the Holl lay below.

My only friend in that company was Jackal, and we didn't share a common tongue. A half a mile below us, spread out over half the small valley, was a siege of a thousand enemy troops. I didn't know the plan, I didn't know if there was one. I was sure, based on the fear rising in my heart, that we didn't have a plan. But there was one, it turned out, and it was a good one.

Four whole companies, each one hundred strong, had split off the night before when the scouts returned with the news. They'd missed the party and missed the ambush and, in white cloaks, crept behind and flanked the enemy, waiting for the signal.

The signal was when we opened fire from the top of the pass with captured gatling guns until we'd spent their ammo, then we charged screaming, skiing down the hill, guns raised. Ponies don't know much about charging down icy slopes, however, and by the time I reached the battle it was over.

Almost over, actually, as it turned out. A stray bullet took down my pony and when I rose, I found myself face to face with a very, very angry man in a green uniform. His saber came down, and I blacked out.

Eighteen

I opened my eyes and the world was hazy, gray, and dim.

"He's awake," said a familiar voice. After a moment, I placed it. Nola.

"Your friend here likes getting stabbed, doesn't he?" Kata asked.

"Last time it was a bullet," Nola replied.

"Close enough," Kata replied. "Good evening, Dimos. Welcome back to the land of the living."

I tried to talk. I was going to say "I was dead?" but as soon as I opened my mouth, searing pain shut me down.

"Don't try to talk or move or breathe too hard," a stranger's voice, a high tenor male voice, said. "You've taken a sword to the face. You can't see because there's gauze over your right eye and... and you don't have your left one."

I felt a hand on mine. Probably Nola's.

"You're going to survive though," the stranger said.

I fell back into the warm blackness.

....

When I woke up again, I was sitting in a chair and surrounded by friends: Sorros and Nola, Grem and Dory, Kata, Joslek, Jackal, even Vin was there. The gauze was gone, and I could see fairly well. There was a paper cone taped over my remaining eye, with the bottom snipped off, leaving me the tiniest field of vision. I had to turn my head to look around.

"That cone's there so you don't move your eye," Nola said. "The nurse told me that when you do, the muscle in your left eye moves too, and I'd say 'it's still healing' if it had started healing yet at all."

"Can I talk?" I tried to ask. I failed.

"And don't talk," Nola said. "And when you *can* talk, maybe tomorrow, the first thing you're going to do is thank Jackal."

"He carried you here," Sorros said, "if you can believe that."

After what I'd been through with the old man, I could.

"I don't know how much you missed," Sorros said. "But, well, I guess I'm going to swallow my pride and say—shit, kid, you just saved us all again. If Karak and their 'Freer Companies' hadn't shown up I don't know what we'd be doing."

"You're in Holl," Nola said.

"Before they pinned us down, we were doing better than we feared," Sorros said. "Better than we expected. But worse than we'd hoped. We had the terrain and the spirit but we were short on supplies and people."

"The backbone of this war," Nola said, "has been goatherds with skis and rifles picking them off every time they peek out from behind their walls."

"But they left in a mass, and they cut us off," Sorros said. "It was looking bad. Now, though... the ammunition, the guns... and by the Mountain the armor! I take back everything bad I've ever said about Karak." He thought a moment. "Half of everything bad I've said about Karak."

"We can keep them pinned down now," Nola said.

Dory stood up and paced around the room. "But our advantage lasts only as long as winter," she said.

"The snows won't melt until June," Sorros said.

"They'll have reinforcements by then," Dory said. "We have to get them now."

"No," Sorros said. "Our only advantage is terrain. We can't give that up and attack them head on."

"Dory might be right," Nola said. "They can sit still and wait for reinforcements. We, on the other hand, just got all we're going to get."

"If we retake Moliknari we can push forward, retake Steknadi," Dory said. "It's a village, but from there we can block both passes into Hron and they won't be able to move in. It's easy to defend."

"We can't set up strong placements," Nola replied. "Not in a guerilla war. If we just build walls, they'll blast them down. We have to stay mobile."

"What would it take to win?" I asked. It hurt like hell, and it was unintelligible, but I had to ask it.

"What?" Nola said.

Dory brought me paper.

"What would it take to win?" I wrote. "Do you need to kill every Imperial soldier? Invade the empire? Assassinate the king? What's the endgame of this war?"

Dory read my question to the group.

"We probably have to ask *you* that," Dory said.

"Ask Nola," I wrote. "I'm just a writer. She's a general."

Dory read it, then laughed, then read it aloud.

"When we were fighting Borolia," she said, "we wanted to conquer it. We wanted to be the ones with an empire. The war went on so long because both sides were convinced that their countries couldn't survive without the subjugation of the other. But before this month, Borolia didn't even know that Hron was here."

"We felt safer that way," Sorros said.

"We *were*, for awhile," Dory said.

"States are like people," Vin said. "The best I understand, most people work like this: if they think they can beat you up and take your shit, they will. Letting them knock you around is a losing strategy. If you stand up to them, most of the time they back off. You just have to actually let them back off. That's the only way to live in peace."

"He's got a point," Nola said. "It's a principle in tactics. You never surround an enemy, not completely. If you put their backs to the wall, they'll fight like demons."

"Didn't the Free Company of the Mountain Heather drive the last invading force up against a cliff and then over it?" Dory asked.

"Well, yeah," Nola conceded. "But that's because we thought we'd get away with it. And besides, Wilder tried to run anyway, if I recall."

Sorros tipped his top hat.

"So we need to kick them hard enough that they run back home," Sorros said, "but not so badly that they want to kill every last one of us?"

"Basically," Nola said. "Unless we're reasonably assured we can entirely destroy them, which I'm sad to say we can't."

"What does this mean to the revolutionists in Tar?" Vin asked.

"If anarchists in Tar have a revolution and call for help," Sorros said, "we'll help. Even if it's suicide. Because maybe states *are* like people, and if so, Hron will act like Hron."

"So..." Dory said. "Frontal assault on Moliknari?"

Sorros sighed, and everyone else smiled.

....

Our proposal went in front of the council the next day, and because I was stuck in the clinic I was spared the eleven hour debate that followed. According to Sorros, it had been easy to convince people to join a frontal assault, but a lot of people had had their heart set on the total annihilation of the invading force. No one had the power to outright ban anyone from circling behind their position and killing anyone who tried to flee, of course, but it was determined in the end that doing so would go against the crux of the plan. There would always be time, people realized, to fight a war of annihilation if His Majesty's troops ever came back. And besides that, the assault itself seemed suicidal enough.

When the plan was in place, runners went out to let all the forts and emplacements know and to recall all the ambushers set along the enemy's line of retreat. Three days were given to the messengers as a head start before the army set off to march. Those days were spent in training and/or debauchery, as best suited each person.

After another night, they let me out of the clinic but told me I was under no circumstances to do anything that might possibly let infection set in, like go to war.

"Grem," I said one evening, catching up with my friend as he left the barracks that had been built of the guest hall. "I've barely heard a word out of you since I got here. Or since before I left Hronople."

He nodded. The youth was gone from his face. He was walking well on his wooden leg.

"How have you been?" I asked.

"You told me once, a million years ago, right after I lost my leg, that there was no afterlife. I don't remember if it was you or me who said it, but we said the only remnant of my friends was the freedom they'd left me."

"Well, I don't think either of us put it as eloquently as that," I said.

"When I joined the Free Company, I wasn't afraid to die because I was a child and because my home had just been destroyed. Then, for a long time, I *was* afraid to die. Or to lose my other leg or something. Now I'm not afraid anymore. I'm going to war again, and this time I'm carrying my friends in my heart. By my life or death, I'll continue their legacy. As long as there's Hron, or honestly, as long as there're anarchists somewhere in this world, then I'll be alive."

I looked at him for awhile.

"I guess that's how I've been," he said. "Everything is so serious now. Everything has such weight. I think, if I get through this, there might be levity again in my life. I hope so."

"I miss adventure hour," I said.

He teared up. I did too, only when I did it, it hurt like hell.

He hugged me, then. No one hugs much in Hron, I realized. When they do it, they mean it.

....

The day before the march I was set up in a chair in the barracks, drinking far too much carsa and trying to make up for it by drinking calming teas. Over the course of the day, practically everyone I'd met in Hron came to see me.

When Varin, the writer from the midwinter festival, came, he sat quite close and I tried not to get swept away by how good he smelled. I also tried, and failed, to not become overly self-conscious about my bandaged face.

"I'm almost jealous of you," he said.

I looked at him.

"I'm sorry, that's a terrible thing to say," he said. "It's just... well, the war is over for you, isn't it? You don't have to ride out in the morning wearing a heavy clay vest and holding a piece of metal designed to murder people. I like to wander, I like adventure, but I genuinely don't know that I have it in me to look a person in the eyes and shoot them. Or more so, to look at a field of carnage and run onto it, hoping I can use my life to leverage more life for those around me."

"You don't have to go," I said. "You're a free man."

"I thought about that," he said, "for a long time. But that's not true. I do have to go. For Hron, yes, but I have to go for myself. I have to go precisely because I *don't know if I have it in me*. I want to be a writer, and at least as much as writers need to know other people, writers need to know themselves. So maybe a few days from now I'll know as well as you know."

I wanted to tell him I didn't know myself, but I wasn't sure if that was honest. I hadn't had enough time to think it through.

"Where's Sakana?" I asked.

"She broke up with me," he said. He started laughing. "Left me for a militiaman. I swear to you, though, that's not what this is about!"

"I believe you," I said. "Take care of yourself. No, to hell with that, take care of your friends and let them take care of you. Do stupid things for them."

"You're twenty-three, about to turn seventy-four," he said, grinning.

"I feel it," I said.

He clasped my hand and then went back to his preparations.

I watched from the chair by the fire as people came and left. Dory brought me mashed turnips and boiled greens, about all I could eat. People cried and drank and boasted and played and stood around nervously. Mol came by and introduced me to his wife Somi.

"Aren't you a glassmaker?" I asked.

"Sure," he said. "But she's going, and I love her more than I love my life. So I'm going."

"Time to put my book learning to use, I guess," Somi said. Both of them were trying to keep up a stoic front. Both of them were terrified.

The whole town was terrified. They were seven thousand marching on nine that sat behind fortifications. It was a death march. The most expensive bluff I'd ever imagined.

Nola stopped by in the early hours of the morning. I hadn't even tried to go to bed. "Write me a speech," she said.

"What?" I asked.

"I've never been any good at speeches," she said. "And I know I'm not a general and I know we're all equals but you know, people look to someone like me before we run in and try to shoot people. And I want something to say to them other than 'shoot anyone who tries to kill me please, also Hron is great.' Because honestly I tried to write something earlier and that's basically what I got."

"Starting with a joke is for politicians," I said. "A good battle speech, from what I figure, is full of earnest superlatives that are, somehow, nonetheless true. A good battle speech is the kind of thing that doesn't make any sense if you're not about to get shot at, if you're not surrounded and outnumbered."

"Got it," she said. "Write me a speech. A short one. I'm going to bed."

I wrote her a speech.

Sorros came last. Only the battle-insomniacs were still awake, speaking in hushed tones in the hall, or reading books, or just staring at the walls.

"You came," I said.

"I came."

He sat next to me, took my hand in his, and we were silent for a long time.

"You saved my life," I told him at last. "You and Nola."

"You've repaid us twice over," he said.

"I just wanted to thank you, is all," I said.

"Believe me when I tell you that you're welcome."

"Are we going to get through this?" I asked.

"Probably not," he said.

"You should be with Nola," I said.

"I'll be with her on the march," he said. "And I can't sleep."

Dammit walked up to us then, wagging her tail, and she laid down across my feet.

"I guess I just want to say that, whatever happens here, I hope you write about us."

"I will," I said.

"Write about us honestly, too. I don't want to see propaganda. We're just people. People have to make informed decisions. Lies won't help with that."

"What was it like, growing up free?"

"I don't have a frame of reference," Sorros said. "I can't imagine anything else. I fought with my moms all the time and I hated hard work and I loved the woods and I loved winter. If I hadn't joined the militia I'd probably have wound up a woodsman, I think. Gathered herbs and mushrooms. That never felt like work, that was a treasure hunt."

He got out of his chair to sit on the floor with Dammit, rubbing her belly.

"I might have lied when I told you I didn't know the accord," he said. "I just didn't want you to get hung up on it. But you've seen this place now. The most important part of the accord came from the villages, not the revolutionists. The most important part is this: 'All people are free. When we speak of freedom, we acknowledge that freedom is a relationship between the people of a society. This relationship of freedom is created by means of mutual respect, the acknowledgment of one another's autonomy, and the ability to hold one another responsible for their actions. All people are free and all people are responsible to themselves and to one another.'

"I feel that to the core of my being. I grew up with it and my great, great, grandmother grew up with it. I can't understand anyone who'd live a different way. I wish I could, but I can't. I'm not even angry at Borolia, not really, because I can't understand them. I've never been angry at a fever. I've never hated a blizzard, or a drought or a famine. They are just things that happen and we fight them."

The first risers were up already, and a handful of people were headed to the kitchens.

"Why are they here?" Sorros asked. He sounded plaintive, childlike. "Why did they invade?"

"They told me it was for the glory of the King," I said, "and maybe for coal and for iron. And that's part of it. But they're here because they're an empire. It's expand or die for them, it's built into the very economy. Class tensions at home are near to bursting. Peace doesn't work."

Sorros gave Dammit one last pat, then stood. "I think I'll help with breakfast," he said. He started to walk away, then came back and hugged me. "I hope your speech is good," he said, then walked away once more.

Nineteen

We are anarchists, and we are immortal. We are the country of ghosts, and we are immortal. We will fight them until we are dead, and our bones will fight them after. The memory of our existence will fight them. We will drive them to Tar, we will drive them to Borol, and in each of their hearts we will brand the memory that those who are free will never yield. Today, let us be ghosts! Today, let us be ghosts!

....

I watched from the battlements as they marched out in the morning, dour and cold and determined. Those who stayed and waved them off did so with tears in their eyes.

I had one hand resting on the wooden wall in front of me, the other on the arm of my chair. I'd declared it mine, made three strangers drag it to the battlement so that I could stand guard. Ekarna would have thrown a fit, but Ekarna was dead, and I figured that if someone took Holl while our army was away, I wouldn't have time to die of infection anyhow. So I sat in my chair under blankets with a rifle and a basket of eggs.

I watched long after they were gone, long into the night, then curled up on blankets to sleep. I woke frigid in the starlight and paced the wall until the sun returned. I kept vigil in my chair the whole of the next day and night. It was the least I could do, I thought. The very least.

Survivor's guilt is a terrible thing, it turns out. In some ways, it would have been easier on my nerves if I'd gone with them. But I had been a bad shot even before some hired colonial thug had cut my dominant eye in half, and with my fresh wound, I would have been more a liability than an asset. Most everyone, at the core of their being, wants to be an asset to their friends and community. If Hron had taught me anything, it had taught me that.

I thought I was going to stay in that chair until news returned, waiting on the widow's walk of the palisade. But the cold and, it must be admitted, boredom came to me eventually and I returned to the warm barracks and lost myself in my writing most days.

I was asleep when the first militia on skis made it back to the wall and inside the gate, but the excitement woke me and I made it to the wall in time to see a thousand people come flooding into the valley from the pass and march back to Holl.

I went down to join the small crowd, those of us who'd stayed, along the main road into town.

"So few?" I said, or maybe someone near me did.

"My friends?" I asked, when I saw Vin and his comrades.

"With the back, guarding the wounded," he answered.

"And...?" I asked.

"Moliknari is ours," he said. "What's left of it."

The news must have reached elsewhere in the crowd at the same time, because a ragged cheer went up. First two voices, then more. Slowly, the grim-faced soldiers joined in, into a tumult of catharsis that hacked away at our throats and burned out the worst of our fears. We had won.

....

"Your speech worked," Nola said. I held her to my breast as she cried. "But Sorros listened too well."

Along with a squadron of the Gray Brigade, my friends had taken the vanguard. Nola, Dory, and Joslek remained. Grem and Sorros did not.

"We said we'd fight them with the bones of our body," Dory said. "And we did."

....

I went into journalist mode to cope, and by the end of the day I'd pieced together the battle.

With the body armor only effective against small arms fire, and the Imperial army equipped with machine guns, it was determined that close-quarters combat was safest. Kata, Habik, Jackal, Bahrit, and a few other munitions experts crept across the snow in white cloaks under the new moon and sapped the walls, first to the front and then to the fore. Habik and Kata were both shot in the process. Habik survived his wound, Kata did not.

The vanguard ran in the front gates from the valley, a distraction, the rest came in the rear, down the mountain. Sorros might have been the second, after Kata, to die on our side, picked off from a tower just after he crossed back into the town of his birth.

The fighting was street to street, building to building. The vanguard, with more trained snipers and more elderly combatants, took a tower and began picking off anyone in the green-and-gold. Grem went down with a bullet in his shoulder—the bullet struck an artery and he died fast and cold. He never did play his concertina again.

Vin and the ex-conscripts took the main square and held it, probably the most important tactical move in the battle. He says it had been Somi's idea. Somi and Mol went down together, cut in half by a gatling gun.

The militia left the front gate unguarded, however, and eventually they forced the army to retreat.

Nearly five hundred stayed, both those too wounded to move and those who committed to rebuilding and refortifying the town. Every widow and widower made on the field that day took a necklace of teeth, and a dying custom was reborn.

The funeral was declared across the whole of Hron and Karak, and for a week, the country mourned, dressed all in white in honor of the new ghosts. I traveled to Moliknari for the ceremony there, the one with the bodies, and at Nola's assistance I helped carry Sorros in a maple coffin into the cave of the dead, into the Mountain, to lay beside his mothers.

The Freer Companies from Karak took some of the heaviest losses—all but the Freer Company of the Hollow, who saw the odds and refused to fight. Representatives from Karak and Hron talked things out, and while of course none could speak on behalf of anyone else, Hron largely agreed to a pact of mutual self defense.

I stuck around for two weeks more, interviewing survivors and helping out as much as anyone would let me. But I was mostly just floating in grief, and I knew I needed to get away. So I left for Hronople.

Twenty

Six months have passed, and the snow has melted in the valleys. The panes have come down off the large greenhouses and I can wear a single long-sleeved longshirt while I work the fields, pruning trees and weeding, fixing irrigation. I might have ridden off the "war hero" prestige for awhile longer, but there's work to be done and it feels good to do it.

Vin and I fell in love, or at least infatuation, on the way back from Sotoris. He changed my bandages every night, applied ointment to my wounds, and cooked me dinner. He's dropped his plans for moving back to Tar to foment revolution, at least for now. I think he's doing it for me, and I suspect in a year or two I'll lose him to that calling. Myself, there's a chance I'll join him in Tar if he'd have me, but I won't be going back to Borol anytime soon. It's full of the wrong kind of memories and it's full of people who'd love to kill me.

Freedom is a relationship between people, and freedom was given to me by Sorros and Ekarna Ralm, by Grem, by Desil Tranikfel. By four thousand women and men from these mountains who died in the war. His Majesty's forces might be back, but they haven't been yet.

I'm happy in Hron. I've got an eyepatch and a wicked scar down my face—Vin says it makes me look tough. I live with Jackal and have been studying Deded. Nola, Dory, and Joslek have found new recruits for the Free Company of the Mountain Heather, including almost a dozen people from Karak. Habik stayed in Moliknari, working to see what he can do about producing firearms, ammunition, and armor without destroying the ecosystem. I haven't seen Sakana or Varin, but I heard they both survived and I hope they've found what they're looking for. Vin spends half his time as a farrier and half his time helping Jackal blow things up, and his friends are quickly becoming my friends.

This book, though, this book isn't for Hron. I'll print it in Hronople, but this book is for the people of Borolia, so that they might know the country their leaders tried to invade. It's for anyone who wants to know that there are ways to relate with one another besides through the authority of economic or political power. It's so that they know that another way of life is possible, that there are people who live it.

Afterword

This book is not a blueprint. This book is not intended to be the be-all and end-all of "what anarchists are looking for." No book should be. I wrote it in a secondary world, and set roughly 150 years in the past, precisely to make it clear that I don't believe "this is what humanity should be doing."

The purpose, as I understand, of utopian fiction isn't to set out the path to freedom, or even to paint a clear picture of freedom, but instead, to offer an argument that freedom is possible. I don't hate dystopian fiction, but frankly I'm a bit bored by it. It's a bit too safe. Utopia is a bit more dangerous, a bit more threatening to the status quo. It certainly requires making yourself more vulnerable as an author because you intend for your work to be critiqued.

There's an irony here because I believe the opposite is true outside of the written word. Saying what you're for is safe. It's perfectly legal in the United States, as an example, to say that you desire to live in an anarchist society. Taking actual steps towards that— or even just directly confronting any of the ills of this society—is rarely so.

Yet, in fiction, we are surrounded by books about "what's wrong," because they're easier to write and sell. That doesn't make dystopia a bad genre—it's an important part of the larger literary world. We just have an awful lot more of it.

I could be wrong about all of this. Maybe I'm exaggerating the importance of utopian fiction and being too harsh on dystopia. I could be wrong about a lot of things.

I could be wrong about everything that's in this book.

In fact, I assume I *am*. Because while this book is not solely the product of my own imagination—many of the practices are ones I've seen developed within antiauthoritarian communities during the two decades or so of my involvement—there just isn't a way we can know what the world we want will look like. Because the world I want is a free world in which individuals and communities figure out, together, what their world will look like. That absolutely precludes the use of the contents of one woman's brain as a blueprint.

This book is not a blueprint.

....

This book is deeply personal—more so than anything I've ever written—despite there not being a single character in here that is anything like a self-insert. I'm not a gay, masculine journalist with a penchant for muckraking. Maybe I see myself the most in Grem, but that just might be because he has a concertina and is confused about his place in the world.

This book is deeply personal because as much as it's not a blueprint, it was the best and clearest way I could say to people "here, this is what I want, this is what I'm fighting for." It had to be fiction because, at the end of the day, what I want isn't really about the economics—who the glassmaker gets his meals from—but instead about the way that people treat one another.

I learned the hard way—or maybe the beautiful way—what it was like to be a foreigner and not particularly well-liked within an anarchist community when I first found myself amongst the squatters in the Netherlands when I was our hero's age. I had the hardest time making friends. Yet, arrested at an antifascist action, a bus full of strangers lied about their nationality in order to keep me from being separated out. Two even went to foreign detention with me, successfully convincing the guards that they too probably weren't Dutch so that I wouldn't be isolated. They didn't do it because they liked me, or got along with me, or were trying to sleep with me, or thought I had anything to offer them at all. They did it because it is what an anarchist does.

Experiences like that have shaped me fundamentally and the best way I could apply my talents to support the work they have done is to write about them by not writing about them. By writing about what we all might aspire to do—take care of one another of our own free will.

I wrote this book in 2013 and it was published during one of the worst periods for my mental and physical health. My brain likes playing tricks on me, like telling me I'm dying. It especially used to like doing that back then. As I lay on a mattress on my friend's floor, convinced I was truly about to pass from this world, all I could think of was *well I wrote this book*.

I no longer see *A Country of Ghosts* as my sole or even primary contribution to the world, but eight years ago, it was. So, it's personal.

....

Looking back, there are aspects of the book I would have written differently, but very few regarding the actual structure or politics. Nothing in the intervening years has done anything but solidify my beliefs in mutual aid and solidarity as the cornerstones of a healthy society. Maybe I would have phrased certain aspects differently. Maybe I would have lengthened some scenes, cut short some others.

Since writing this book I've learned a lot more about the subtle (and non-subtle) ways that orientalism creeps into western culture. I worked hard, when writing this book, to avoid falling into easy, lazy world-building by mapping cultures too hard to existing cultures (though of course Borol is fairly British, let's be honest, as one of the arch-typical colonial states). I could have worked harder. I don't know to what degree I succeeded, to what degree I failed.

When the first edition of this book came out, I did a speaking tour about anarchism and utopian fiction. At one stop, an Indigenous anarchist heard me out, then said simply, "this continent was colonized and destroyed by people looking for utopia." I've thought about that ever since.

If there's a single complicated issue I have with Hron and this book, it's the simplicity with which I present the influx of refugees and the creation of Hron as a political entity. The book is about resisting colonization, yet it relies on the trope of a willing Indigenous population and empty land that can be settled and worked by the refugee population. In my study of history and colonization, I do believe that this is a reasonable thing to present and is distinct from colonization. Numerous times, societies have accepted a large influx of people who have brought some of their own culture and created syncretic, non-colonial societies (or assimilated wholesale into the society they've entered). I'm sure each of those times, it's been messier than history would leave us to believe. Yet it stands in sharp contrast to the project of colonization, displacement, extraction and genocide.

I didn't address that complexity in this book. I hope one day I'm able to return to the Cerrac mountains, perhaps with a prequel, and certainly with a lot more research and a lot more conversation teasing out these distinctions.

It's especially dangerous to pair utopianism with the idea of empty space. The idea that there are parts of the world we can disappear to and set up our little perfect societies is always and forever a misguided one and one that has fed into some of the worst atrocities in history. Working for a better society is worth doing. We need to do it where we are or where we're wanted. We also, frankly, need to earn it. We can't just ignore the awful shit of the world and start anew. We need to fix the awful shit. The act of fixing the awful shit is the only way we'll get a sense of how to do what we want to do in the first place.

....

If we need to tell ourselves there is a shiny silver city just over the next hill, we do so because we need the courage to keep walking, and we need a direction to walk. Utopia should serve more as a compass than a map. It tells us which way to walk. It doesn't tell us what we'll run across on the path and it doesn't tell us what it'll be like when we get there. It just says "we need to walk towards freedom." With freedom, of course, being something we give one another.

It's the journey, not the goal, that matters. The only purpose of the goal is to enrich the journey and give it direction. A hundred years ago, anarchist Errico Malatesta said, "the subject is not whether we accomplish Anarchism today, tomorrow, or within ten centuries, but that we walk towards Anarchism today, tomorrow, and always."